MINDFIELD

C.W. JAMES

MINDFIELD

Copyright © 2023 by C.W. James.

This book is a work of fiction. Names, characters, businesses, organizations, places, events and incidents either are the product of the author's imagination or are used fictitiously. Any resemblance to actual persons, living or dead, events, or locales is entirely coincidental.

For information contact:

Insundry Productions Books

Gardnerville NV 89460

insundryproductions.com

Cover design by Miblart.com

ISBN (ebook): 978-1-7368013-9-0

ISBN (paperback): 978-1-7368013-8-3

Library of Congress Control Number: 2023904820

Also by C.W. James

The Treasure of Peril Island
Brothers Three

Chapter One

... LOOK AT THAT damn TSA line...

... Gate 15A? Where the hell is...

... what did she pack in this thing...

Matt Storm stood at the airport, arms rigid by his sides, fists clenched, as swarms of people pushed past, their thoughts carpet-bombing him. His dad's voice cut through the cacophony, "Matt, are you listening to me?"

"Yeah, yeah, sure." Matt's voice was a low monotone. He shuffled slightly to his left, creating an extra foot of distance between him and his parents to shield himself from the added burden of hearing their unspoken thoughts as he attempted to concentrate on his father's words only. He'd found that method kept things simple when dealing with them—or with anyone else, for that matter. Keep people a safe distance away. Unfortunately, in the crowded airport, the sheer number of folks rushing by forced an endless stream of their random thoughts into his brain like overstuffed passengers on a rush-hour bus.

"Are you feeling all right, dear?" his mother asked with concern.

"No worries." Matt managed a smile. *If these other people around me would either go away or stop thinking.*

"We could give Dr. Bradford a call..." she went on.

The last person Matt wanted to talk to... his former therapist. Correction: one of his former therapists. "I have his number on my phone. I'll call him if I think I'm going into crisis," Matt assured her. "You can trust me to do that."

Matt got along fine with his parents after he'd allowed himself to be 'cured' following years of therapy. They were relieved about that, of course, but still worried about him, appearing a little afraid of him. Sometimes their body language reflected this unease, turning slightly away from him as though ready to flee, or the expression in their eyes as they analyzed his every word and movement for signs of a relapse. Most of the time, he knew their anxiousness from their thoughts; waiting—expecting, perhaps—for some sign of a return trip to crazy town. Although Matt had long mastered the art of quickly adjusting to their thoughts to calm them down, it was getting old.

"Perhaps we have time to buy another ticket..." His mother turned to his father.

Matt rolled his eyes. He had been plagued for nine years with the unwanted ability to read the minds of complete strangers if they came within three feet of him. That was bad enough, but to be bombarded with thoughts in a language he couldn't understand would drive him out of his freaking skull. He had picked up from his mother's mind that she was hoping this trip would be like a 'second honeymoon' for his parents, so he'd casually suggested that they should go by themselves, hinting how much more romantic it would be without him tagging along—not to mention cheaper, which his father appreciated. "This cruise is all for you guys. I'll be fine on my own. I'm going out to backpack for a night. That's my vacation."

"He's right, Laura, it's you and me and the Greek Isles," Dad put his arm around her, "And I'm sure Matt wants to be alone here so he can throw some wild parties, eh, Matt?" His father's tone was light, but with more than a whisper of hope that his son would do something unexpected like that.

"I'll never tell," Matt responded with a grin.

"Come on, hon, the security line isn't getting any shorter," Dad urged. He shook Matt's hand. "See you in two weeks, Matt."

"Remember to do your mindfulness exercises," his mother added, "and the mediation."

"I will." *Like never.* Matt turned his cheek to receive a kiss from his mother. "Bon voyage."

The group exchanged waves, and Matt watched his parents disappear into the security area. When they were out of sight, he frantically dug out his ear buds and jammed them in.

... why are we going...

... another gate change...

... I hope that screaming kid isn't...

Matt cranked up the volume on his phone, the music almost successful in drowning out the crowd's thoughts. He pushed his way through them, intent on the single goal of getting out of that place as fast as he could. It was like he was maneuvering his way through a bizarre, backwards minefield, where he was a moving explosive that could blow up by colliding with an obstacle—another mind.

He picked up his pace, rapidly threading his way through the travelers dragging their suitcases behind them like petulant children. At last, stepping outside the terminal, he realized he had held his breath as he made his way to the exit. Exhaling, he caught the traffic light and quickly reached his father's car. Pulling out the ear buds, he unlocked the door and climbed inside. After the airport chaos, the car interior was quiet. The 'thoughtscape,' as he referred to the random thoughts careening through his head, had taken on the welcomed, calm characteristics of a glassy, smooth pond.

The drive home from the airport sent Matt's stress levels down, though he still felt a tight knot lingering in his chest from the onslaught of thoughts he'd received at the terminal. A hike through the peace of the nearby national forest would help; it always did.

He placed a couple of cans of food on the kitchen counter, along with a note to the neighbor girl who was going to feed their family cat, Sushi, while he was gone overnight. Climbing into his old car, showing its age with its cracked windshield, bald tires, and 'watch out for falling parts' bumper sticker, he drove up the winding mountain pass, sighing with relief when his ancient vehicle reached the top. He snagged a place in the busy parking lot and patted his car's transmission tunnel like it was a faithful horse. He got out and put on his backpack. With a relieved sigh, savoring the solitude he was about to experience, he set off down the trail to one of his favorite spots to camp.

The next morning, Matt finished his breakfast as he sat by his tent. His campsite, a small clearing ringed by the thick forest, the mighty trees acting like guards, was located off a lightly used trail. The area was empty, save for his tent and small camp stove. A cool breeze rustled through the leaves, leaving him content.

He put down his mess kit, stood, and stretched. The woods had performed their wizardry again. The quiet and isolation had pushed all the tension from the onslaught of other people's thoughts from his mind, leaving a blissful calm. He strolled to the edge of the area with a smile. The still morning air was crisp with the sharp, almost antiseptic, odor of pine, and the scent of sap drying on sun-warmed wood wafting in. To the south and west, the jagged outline of the mountain ridges against a cloudless sky.

Nice morning, isn't it?

The thought rocketed into his mind from nowhere. Matt jumped, and his breathing became anxious and shallow. He cast a glance back to his tent and instinctively reached out to grab one of its metal support rods, as though he needed to ground himself. The voices left him alone out there. They'd never followed him so far out before. That was why he camped and hiked by himself as often as he could.

Sorry, dude, didn't mean to startle you.

Matt circled the campsite, his footsteps breaking the morning quiet around him. His eyes darted from tree to tree, hoping that he was wrong and that someone else was there. But with every passing minute, it became more and more clear: he was completely alone.

His brain filled with all the doubts and fears he had kept at bay for years. Could all of his head doctors be correct? Were the voices he heard in his mind figments of his imagination, the mark of a slow descent into insanity? Or were they the actual thoughts of other people he could pick up? He'd long believed that. No, that opened the possibility of error. He corrected himself: he long knew he could read the thoughts of others. Problem was, there was no mind to read now because nobody was near him.

He felt a chill run down his spine as he circled back to the original question. Was he losing his grip on reality? He rejected that idea immediately.

No, there was some other explanation. There had to be. There must be.

"Who are you? Where are you?" he called.

Dense bushes and trees hemmed in this small pocket of space. Matt couldn't see anything beyond the edge of his campsite. The undergrowth was so thick it could conceal an entire football team. He turned in a complete circle, his eyes moving from tree to tree, between them, along the ground, searching for the source of the invading thought.

The silence in his skull was total and unnerving. Matt stopped, shutting his eyes and tilting his head like a puzzled German Shepard, concentrating on locating the other voice again. His mind picked up nothing.

A hand dropped on his shoulder.

Matt cried out and spun around.

A guy, perhaps two or three years older than him, stood behind him. He smiled and stuck out his hand. "Trent Spencer."

Matt hesitated a second, then warily shook. "Matt Storm."

There was an awkward pause.

"I never expected to find another one out here, in the middle of the woods." Trent jammed his hands into his jeans pockets as he took in the view.

"Another what?" Matt asked cautiously.

Trent nodded toward Matt and grinned. "Another telepath, of course."

Chapter Two

MATT STAGGERED BACK A few steps, almost like he had been slugged. He checked Trent up and down. The two were six feet tall. The visitor had wavy blonde hair and a square jaw. In fact, his entire head consisted of distinct angles. He looked like a movie cowboy, wearing jeans, boots, and a black t-shirt snug against a muscular torso and arms. They were working muscles, not of a gym rat, a marked contrast to Matt's slender build.

Matt suddenly realized Trent's thoughts were a complete blank to him.

Trent must have noticed the confusion. He grinned as though at a private joke, then reached into one pocket. Rapidly, Trent's mind became clear, and Matt could read his thoughts.

"You're like me," Matt whispered in amazement. Waves of conflicting emotions smashed into him: relief, anxiety, fear, joy. The feelings swirled down to a single thought: Trent was another telepath. It was as if he had been an alien stranded in a strange world for seventeen years and had now encountered one of his own kind out of nowhere. At the same time, he felt naked, his mind exposed. He backed to three feet from Trent.

"Is that your distance, your limit? About three feet?" Trent didn't wait for a response. "Mine's five."

Matt placed himself another two feet back.

Trent held up his hands and laughed. "Whoa, dude, whoa. I don't want you to back into the next county. Do you really want to communicate this way? The OG way? I mean, actually talking? We don't have to, you know."

Matt nodded. "Yeah. Yeah, I do. Call it a force of habit."

"Fine by me." Trent shrugged and pointed at the coffee pot resting on the camp stove. "May I? Smells great."

Matt gestured *go ahead*.

The visitor slipped off his backpack, poured himself a cup of coffee, and sat down. "Go on, have a seat. This is your camp, after all. Don't worry, my rabies shot is current."

Matt sat cross-legged on the ground, four feet away. Trent appeared calm and affable, although some underlying tension existed, not only in his posture but flowing out from his body as well. Perhaps it was the way he clutched the tin cup, or that his eyes constantly darted around.

His visitor blew on the hot brew a couple of times and sipped. He took in the view approvingly. "I understand why you enjoy being out here. So peaceful, so quiet. No cars, no phones, no barking dogs ..."

"No other people's thoughts," Matt added.

The two locked eyes. Trent nodded after taking another drink. "No other people's thoughts," he responded evenly.

Matt gasped audibly and leaned forward as he noticed his Trent's eyes. Matt's eyes were a pale, almost colorless, blue. Trent's were the same color as his, exactly. Trent gave a half-smile. Matt flushed with embarrassment as he straightened up. "Sorry, I didn't mean to stare. I never have seen that color of eyes on anybody else. Not my parents or even any other person in my family," he explained lamely. "Nobody except you."

"This may be a genetic marker," Trent said as tapped an index finger under his left eye.

"A genetic marker?"

"Of our ... talent, shall we call it?" Trent smiled, a knowing grin between two people who shared an insider's secret. "But I'm not sure. You're the only other telepath I've run into."

"You too," Matt fumbled over his words as his thoughts jammed up. "I thought I was the only one—I mean, the only real one. Like, other than some in the movies, but that's phony ... either I was the only true one, or I was ..." his voice trailed off.

"Crazy?" Trent finished. "I understand that feeling. Hearing people's voices when they aren't talking, and all that? Most people find that a little weird."

"Man, if you only knew," he paused, "Maybe you do." Matt figured if anyone would understand him, it would be Trent. Finally, somebody he could confide in and stop pretending to be what he wasn't. His words spurted out, his voice suddenly intense and edged with urgency. "I mean, I can see into people's minds. Someone else's thoughts pop up in my head, whether I want them to or not. I hear them like the birds singing or cars going by. I pick up my mom making up grocery lists. I answer questions before I'm asked."

He leaned forward and stabbed his index finger in the dirt for emphasis. "The worst part is if I tell anybody else that I understand their thoughts, they stare like I have three heads sprouting out of my neck and little green monsters are dancing in my hair. They looked at me like something was wrong with *my* mind, but what they have in *their* heads is what was wrong. People want me to understand that kind of thing isn't real because it doesn't make sense or because it makes them uncomfortable or because it means they have to change how they think. The truth is they exist, these voices, these thoughts in my head."

Matt tried to stop his words, but he might as well have tried to halt the ocean tide with his bare hands. "Hear talking in your head? I tell you I can read minds? Well, off to the neurologist I go. I could have a tumor or some other nasty thing growing in my skull. After all that checks out negative, next stop: the shrinks. They perch in their fancy high-backed leather chairs, fingers tented together, like ... like some all-knowing god. Here, tell me, when did you first think when you started hearing these voices? Was it around puberty? What do they say to you? Are they speaking to you now? Are they giving you commands? Do you remember potty training? So, I tried to pretend I made the whole thing up as a joke. Somehow that makes everything worse. I mean, come on! I wouldn't make up something nutty like that unless I honestly had something seriously wrong upstairs."

Agitated now, Matt jumped to his feet. "First visit this shrink, then that one, and the other two floors up. No progress? There's always another one, the next flight up. Here, lie down, make yourself comfortable. Here, have some pills. These cute little blue ones will shut those unpleasant voices up. But they don't stop them because the voices I'm hearing in my head aren't fake, but real.

Theirs. *Their* thoughts. I don't want them, but there they are, sucking up space in my brain. My parents give each other worried looks about me, their nut-case kid. They didn't sign up for this. Skinned knees, a broken leg perhaps, but not this. Not a fruit-bat crazy child. A tumor would have been better. At least that could be cut out, a precise physical explanation, tying up everything in a sleek, tidy package."

"At last I figured out how to have some peace, get all these people away from me. I finally allowed myself to be cured." He threw his arms wide and shouted the word to the sky. "Hallelujah! The head doctors and the pills—which I flushed down the toilet or pocketed in my mouth—work. Ta-da! Look at me! I'm a success story in the world of modern mental health treatment." Matt sat again and released a lengthy breath. "Man, oh man. That was really, really excellent. I've never been able to tell that to anybody else. Ever." He flashed an embarrassed smile. "Sorry about the drama."

Trent shook his head and grinned. "No worries. It seemed like it needed to be aired out."

"The vintage has been bottled a long time." Matt shook his head and grinned back. "I guess you understand."

"I grew up on a cattle ranch in the high desert," Trent said. "Lots of, um, can we say, interesting people live out there. Get this." He smiled and counted off on his fingers. "Healing from crystals, getting a massage based on the polarities from the earth's magnetic field, folks building bunkers to survive the newest trendy mega-disaster leading to the utter breakdown of civilization. I mean, the couple on the next parcel to the north built a landing pad for UFOs. Lights and everything. No joke. It wasn't unusual for me to say I was telepathic."

"I guess not."

They both laughed.

Trent gestured toward Matt. "So you're in high school? A, what ..."

Matt nodded. "Senior this coming year. I suppose you're in college."

"Was." Trent glanced behind Matt's shoulder for a second as if he saw something, or expected to, before returning his gaze to Matt. "Was in college."

"I guess you didn't like it."

"No, I liked it fine." Trent chuckled. "Pretty easy to un-cover what the professors wanted. I simply sat in the front row and spat their thoughts back at them. They ate it up with a spoon. I just confirmed their high opinion of themselves. Of course, I also found out what they thought of the students. Really ugly."

Matt laughed as well. "I try to sit near the smart kids at school. Makes taking tests a cinch. I have a great GPA, no study or effort required. So why did you leave college?"

Trent shook his head. "I had reasons."

Matt waited for Trent to elaborate. He didn't. Questions tumbled into Matt's mind like clothes off a shelf, endless and overstuffed, overwhelming his ability to ask them. "I always wondered what I would say, or ask, if I met another ... telepath ... but now, I just can't think ..." He was silent for a second. "Hey, how many are there? Of us, I mean, our... kind, with our ... power," Matt groped for words. "Like, I thought I was some freak of nature. Instead, you're like me... or me like you. Our telepathy is only another part of us. Like hands or thumbs or the facility to remember things that never happened or the thrill of seeing your name in print for the first time." Matt burst out laughing. "I don't even know what I'm talking about."

Trent sat calmly, waiting in his own space, peering into Matt's eyes and watching the young man's excitement boil over.

Matt relaxed and finished, "Like, we can't be the only ones out of billions on earth. There has to be more."

"There must be. The probability is too large that there aren't. But how many?" Trent spread his hands. "Tens? Hundreds? Who knows?"

"So I'm not alone," Matt was as relaxed and happy as he had been for years. "There are others!" he shouted at his sudden outburst of happiness. He grinned broadly and giggled like a child.

"Trouble is, there isn't any way to meet them," Trent said. "You would only discover another telepath by walking past them. It's random, like my running into you."

"Hey, I got an idea!" Matt exclaimed. "Let's hold a convention! We could post on the internet that all telepaths—"

"No!" Trent barked out as a command, cutting him off. He stiffened and leaned toward Matt, his eyes blazing. He emphasized his words, jabbing his finger. "No! Don't let them find out!" After a second, he simmered down, collected himself, and sat back. "Not a good idea."

"Okay, okay. Scratch the convention," Matt said, a little surprised at the reaction to his joke. There was a moment of silence. "Hey, when did you notice you could do ... it?"

"Hmm?" Trent's mind seemed to be elsewhere, as though Matt's gag had pulled up terrible memories. "About seven or eight, I think."

"Me too, me too," Matt went on excitedly. "I couldn't get a complete picture of what they were thinking. Then I got older, and I started hearing their actual words."

Trent nodded. "Same here. Telepathy must be like language or motor skills. It develops as you grow up."

A thought suddenly occurred to Matt. "Wait a minute. How did you sneak up on me? I mean, tough to do to a telepath. Can you do some kind of mind trick, like hypnosis or something, to make your mind blank?"

Trent shook his head and pulled a small instrument out of his right pocket. Not a great deal bigger than a deck of cards, it looked like a sophisticated piece of military espionage equipment, something Matt would see on a television show. It was made of a deep black plastic, with a switch on one side.

"I used this. A neuro-pulsamic-jammer."

"A what?"

"Neuro-pulsamic-jammer," Trent repeated. "The idea behind it is relatively simple. It broadcasts all the waves the human brain produces—alpha, beta, theta, delta, gamma, lambda. Think of it as a fan. When a fan is running, it creates white noise, it generates a bunch of sound frequencies that block out other noise. This does the same thing. Masks out all the neural noise. Telepaths can't hack through the interference, either way."

Matt got to his knees and pointed at the jammer. "Dude, I want that. I need that. To stop all those people's thoughts from taking up my head space. Where can I get one?"

Trent stopped Matt with a raised hand. "This is it. The one and only." He turned the device in his hand as he looked at it. "I don't even understand how it works. I mean, I know the principle, but how it does what it does ..." He shook his head.

"How did you get it?"

"Well, it doesn't, in fact, belong to me," Trent admitted.

"Somebody gave it to you?"

Trent shook his head.

"In other words, you stole it." Matt sat back.

"Let's say I possess it through an extended, unauthorized loan." Trent grinned, then drank some more coffee. "And I probably used it too long already," he spoke quietly and rapidly as he pushed the button on the device and stuffed it into a pocket again, glancing around nervously.

In his eagerness to see the gear, Matt got up and moved towards Trent. "At least let me look at it before you put it away. Maybe I can work out—"

"No. Stay out of range. The jammer is turned off. I've thought of them. You can read my mind and find out." He got up and stumbled into a tree. He held out his palms, shaking his head. "No, dude, no, seriously, back off."

Matt stopped, then retreated backwards about six feet, hands up in surrender. "Okay, dude, chill, chill. Weren't you all about not communicating the old-school way?" He pointed to Trent's pocket where he put the jammer. "Why did you say you used it too long? Is it dangerous? Radioactivity or something?"

Trent shook his head, then anxiously looked behind himself, as though he caught a noise in the brush. "No, not radiation. They can trace it," he said in a low voice.

He turned his attention back to Matt. "When I thought of them, they came to the top of my mind. If you get too close, you might read who they are. That may be ... may not be good for you to know." Trent shrugged and sat. He picked up the coffee cup as if had nothing happened.

"Who are *they*?" Matt asked. "A rogue group in the government? The ever-popular evil multinational corporation?"

Trent said nothing.

Matt nodded and sat down again. "Okay," he said, knowing he wouldn't get a reply to any more questions.

A sharp noise rustled the trees to his left. Trent tensed, almost standing once more.

"Just a pine cone falling," Matt said.

Trent gave an anxious smile. "Yeah, yeah, of course."

Matt didn't have to read Trent's mind to see that he had abruptly become more skittish, like a young colt. He was trying to maintain a devil-may-care attitude while expecting Satan to jump out of the earth at any moment to demand his soul.

Trent drained his cup, put it down, and stood. He held out his hand. The suddenness of the move took Matt by surprise, and he climbed to his feet less than gracefully. He stepped forward and took Trent's hand.

Squeezing Matt's hand tightly, Trent stared into his eyes. Matt received a thought from Trent, aimed as if by a laser: *the key is under the bed liner*.

Matt frowned. "What? What—"

"Nice meeting you." Trent released Matt's hand and snatched up his backpack. He quickly backed a few feet and pointed at Matt. "Stay safe, dude, stay safe." Trent turned and plunged back into the forest like an airline passenger making a tight connection.

Matt stared after Trent until he couldn't follow his movement anymore. He stood mutely in the morning sun's warmth, then shivered as he recalled Trent's parting words.

Stay safe, dude, stay safe.

Chapter Three

MATT CHANGED INTO HIS running shoes and shorts, and he took off for a jog around his neighborhood. It was a peaceful area; the homes were spaced far apart and set back from the road. The wind blew in gently from the north, carrying the scent of pine and flower blossoms. The solitude and repetitive action of running completely relaxed him. He even briefly considered joining the cross-country squad during the next school year.

Soon, his thoughts about his recent meeting—no, that word didn't describe what had happened accurately, but it would have to do—a day ago with Trent returned to mind. Matt had an instant connection with Trent, and would have, even if they didn't share the same power. Trent was rugged, strong, and genuine, everything Matt would want in a big brother. Everything he wanted to be.

The encounter also made Matt happy because he wasn't alone. He was not a freak of nature, a peculiar outlier. There had to be more telepaths. Matt lived in a mid-sized city, so perhaps he passed other ones walking down the street every day without recognizing them—or they he.

He realized that couldn't be so; once he walked past another with his skill, they would identify each other, as Trent did with Matt. When he'd, at last, moved towards

Trent, into his range, his mind had instantly picked up Trent's telepathic skills, along with the weird message about a key.

"The key is under the bed liner," Matt mumbled to himself. What does that mean? What key? Why did Trent purposefully send the message so Matt could pick it up? Not to mention what was up with the whole 'stay safe dude' thing?

Matt turned back into his own front lawn and walked around, shaking out his arms. Other questions arose. What about that device Trent said he stole? Was it possible to track the gizmo? The entire business made about as much sense to him as algebra. With a frustrated growl, he vigorously raked his fingers back and forth through his collar-length black hair.

Matt sighed and shook his head. "Perhaps I'm an alien refugee in the center of an interplanetary war, and Trent is a soldier in the army sent to eliminate me before I share the location of our planet with the rest of the galaxy, and he pretended to be like me." He laughed, shaking his head. "I'm playing way too many video games."

He scooped out an assortment of letters from the mailbox, including a catalog from a university he hadn't contacted. More of his parents' handiwork, he supposed. He hadn't decided if he wanted to go to college. Apparently, they had.

Matt went inside and showered. After he dressed, he saw the notification on his cell phone. He punched up the waiting text message and grinned as he read the video game challenge from Hunter. Matt answered in the affirmative.

Hunter was Matt's only real friend, the only person he was comfortable being around. Not only did they like the same stuff, or have the same opinions, but they did the same things and knew the same people. Like Matt, Hunter got good grades, kept his nose clean, and worked hard at whatever he tried. You got what you saw with Hunter. He didn't care what people thought of him. Matt wished he could feel the same.

Hunter was half-a-head shorter, wore black round-rimmed glasses, and sprouted wild, out-of-control, sandy blonde hair, curly enough to scrub a skillet. His eccentricities—like wearing thrift shop suits to school every day paired with bright, ugly ties—put him firmly in the arty clan of kids; in Hunter's case, a member of the drama faction. Matt's friend excelled at improvisation; the only problem Matt had was waiting to laugh until Hunter said something funny, not when he read the upcoming comment in his mind.

Matt drove over to Hunter's house. The two entered the family room, and Matt sat a good three feet away from his friend. If he stayed any closer, it would be cheating. Matt kept his telepathy a closely guarded secret since he figured nobody would want to be friends with someone who could read their minds. Trent was the only other person who knew about his abilities. Matt grinned to himself. It was almost like he was a superhero, his true identity secret to all but—

"Prepare to be annihilated, dweeb, ground into fine silicon dust." Hunter scooped up one controller and tossed the other one to Matt.

Matt easily caught it in one hand. "Keep dreamin' that dream, loser. You're going down so hard, CalTech all the way in California will record an earthquake."

The game started. They grinned, grimaced, and gasped, shouting over the other and swearing at each other, groaning when things didn't go their way and cheering when they did. Matt relaxed completely, even though he was physically tense—hunching over the controller wasn't the most comfortable way to sit. His thumbs were sore from hitting the buttons repeatedly, but he didn't mind. Playing video games was the only time he felt normal.

Both Hunter and Matt cheered and let out whoops as the level ended, throwing their arms into the air in victory. They leaned back in their chairs, their voices coming fast as they talked over each other about game play, who had done best and better, who would take which role next time.

Finally, Hunter rose.

"We will now take a short intermission. Potty break before the next level," he announced. He pointed at Matt. "You want a fizzy sugary drink from the snack bar to rot your teeth?"

Matt smiled as he also got to his feet and stretched. "Yeah. Sounds like a great way to ruin my health."

Hunter assumed the posture of a butler and put on an English accent. "I shall return with your refreshments anon, sir." He bowed and left.

"Remember, shaken, not stirred!" Matt shouted after Hunter. He noticed a new thought process after taking a few steps. At first he dismissed it as Hunter but soon realized he was mistaken. What he was picking up couldn't be his friend; he was out of the room. Something different called to him. Whatever it was, it existed just at the border of his consciousness like a moth fluttering at the edge of a flashlight beam.

He couldn't distinguish exactly what the thought was, only the presence of one, a whisper on the wind. Matt had never encountered something similar before, yet it appeared recognizable. The pattern seemed to repeat itself. Matt couldn't be sure what was looping: his consciousness, the universe ... or both.

Matt looked around the family room, trying to pinpoint the source. He closed his eyes and concentrated, but he couldn't tell what he was picking up on. The brain wave—or whatever—didn't change. It repeated, repeated, repeated, becoming as irritating as listening to a single, high-pitched note played on a violin. Matt shook his head to clear the sensation, but with no success.

He paced back and forth, his mind assaulted by nails across a chalkboard, screeching on and on, vibrating the nerves in his brain. He held his hands over his ears but couldn't block out the feeling. If the damn thing would simply stop, or change at least ...

He faced the television. It displayed the game's pause screen. The console's dull green light blinked on and off, staring balefully back at him from the other side of the room.

Pause ... waiting ... not changing ...

The console was the source, he realized. Somehow, the unthinking calculations of the computer chip were ending up in his brain. He remembered what Trent theorized about telepathy development increasing with age. Had Matt's skill grown to the level of reading the thoughts of inanimate objects?

Matt groaned inwardly. *Does this mean I will hear what the microwave is thinking?*

He must have picked up the game machine's program, but how? He had been next to it most of the time today. When the console was in Hunter's room, Matt had been sitting farther away. To test his theory, Matt backed a few steps. The irritating, repeating message seemed to recede somewhat. He moved toward the console to see if it would strengthen.

Another thought interfered.

What is he doing, trying to communicate with it?

"What are you doing, trying to communicate with it?" Hunter's voice came from behind Matt. "You want it to give you extra lives or something?"

Matt accepted the can of soda. "Worth trying. Maybe I have the power." He waved his free hand toward the console like a wizard.

Hunter dismissed him with a laugh and returned to his seat. He picked up his controller. "Sometimes I wonder about you, dude."

Matt sat as he popped open the cola and sipped. Hunter was out of range now, so he wasn't sure what thoughts ran through his head. Matt tried to remain casual. "Wonder what?"

Hunter shrugged a reply and took the console off pause. The two dived back into the game.

A scream seared through Matt's head. Where it came from—inside or outside his brain—he didn't know. He sprang to his feet, dropping the controller. It clattered loudly on the tiles, and he blinked at it. The sound of the controller's fall echoed throughout the room, bouncing off the walls in multiples. His heart slammed in his chest, and he lowered his gaze, staring at the floor while he tried to make sense of what he had heard. A scream from the screen during a game was nothing new. But that one ... it had been real.

"What's wrong? Matt?" Hunter put down his controller and stood. It was clear from his expression he hadn't heard anything. "Are you alright?"

A second scream spun Matt around. A thought rammed into his brain like a runaway locomotive: someone was in trouble. Another one followed.

A desperate cry broke through, *Matt, I need your help, Matt.*

Hunter came over to Matt and gripped him by the shoulders. "Are you okay? Do you want a doctor or something?"

Hunter's concern flashed into his mind, interfering with the other thought. Matt shoved Hunter out of his way and stumbled into the hallway. He leaned against the wall, closed his eyes, and tried to figure out what the hell was going on, to tune in to the message.

Who is this? Trent? Trent? Is that you? Where are you?

Matt turned slowly in a circle, trying to get a fix on the thought like he was searching for a stronger wireless signal. Despite the initial strength, the message rapidly became scratchy, then thin, as though it had spent all its power just to reach him.

Matt, help, I'm ...

Some kind of static washed over the thought, drowning out the communication. Then it vanished. Matt slumped, dropping his hands to his sides, and swore. He took a deep breath and opened his eyes.

Hunter stood in the doorway, his arms outstretched, looking ready to catch Matt if he keeled over, a worried look on his face. Even though he stood out of range, Matt could tell that Hunter's concern was genuine, not the scared-concern of his parents.

"Are you okay, dude?" Hunter asked.

Matt nodded and managed a weak smile. "Yeah. I only ..." his voice trailed off. What could he say? Another telepath had just communicated to him a call for help? "I must have gotten a little sick."

"Do you need something? To sit down? A glass of water or something?"

"Yes to sitting, no to a drink."

Matt rubbed his neck, went back into the family room, and flopped on the sofa, Hunter hovering behind. Matt had never received a thought like that. Its intensity drained him like he had been swimming against a rip-tide. Hunter moved after another moment and sat on the ottoman, with Matt shifting a little to stay out of range. Neither said anything for a few moments while they caught their breaths. Matt knew he owed Hunter some kind of explanation, but he needed some time to provide one.

"When I was camping," Matt started, "I met this guy—his name was Trent—on the trail. We talked for, I don't know, five, ten minutes, then he moved on." Like afraid of something or somebody, Matt recalled, and, based on the scream he just heard, maybe with reason. "Just now, I got this strong ..." he almost said *thought*, but stopped, at a loss for what to say.

After a second, Hunter offered, "Premonition?"

That word was as good as any. Matt nodded. "Yeah, yeah, like a premonition, a heavy one, that he was in danger, in trouble, hurt. He needed my help."

"Do you believe it? That the whole thing was real, I mean. It didn't come from, like, your imagination? You're not having ... you've told me about all the doctors and all that ..." Hunter said cautiously.

"No worries," Matt smiled at his friend. "I'm not losing it."

"Did something in the game trigger it?" Hunter spoke without a hint of the cold, professional you-really-understand-it's-not-true tone his former therapists had used.

Matt shook his head. "Oh, no, it was there, man. Absolutely in real life."

"So, what are you going to do?" Hunter asked after a pause.

Matt sat quietly for a moment. He spread his hands. "I have no choice. I have to help. Like, I don't know him that well, yeah, but, he's," he stopped himself from saying *one of my kind*, "a cool dude. I can't just blow it off, like, 'I don't know you all that good, so I don't care, go ahead and drown.' How could I live with myself? I have to find him and try to help him," he concluded with equal parts of determination and puzzlement. "But I have no clue how."

It was Hunter's turn to be silent. Suddenly, he clapped his hands once and stood. "Okay, let's roll."

"Let's?" Matt got up to move into Hunter's range. He was relieved his friend's thoughts about joining him were sincere, even excited.

"Yeah, you and me, together. Like Frank and Joe!" He struck a theatrical poise. He noticed Matt's puzzled expression. "You know, *The Hardy Boys*?"

"Who?"

Hunter put his fists on his hips and clucked his tongue. "Dude, you ain't got no culture know-how." Hunter did a mock sigh, then spoke like the voice from movie trailers. He raised one finger. "The Hardy Boys solve thrilling cases, but only after school hours, and during what appears to be long or very frequent vacations, that is. You never checked the bookcase in my room, did you?"

Matt could not help but laugh. "No, I haven't."

"Of course not. Your reading never moved past 'Look, look. See Spot'. I have a complete set of the Hardy Boys. The old ones. Printed in the 1960s. Took me years to find them in thrift stores."

"So what would Fred and Jack—"

"Frank and Joe," Hunter corrected.

Matt waved one hand. "Whatever. What would they do first?"

Hunter tapped his lips with tented fingers, doing his best pondering scientist impersonation. "Ask their famous detective father, Fenton Hardy, for advice."

"Well, we can't do that."

"True," Hunter admitted.

Matt turned serious again. "What then—"

Hunter snapped his fingers, silencing him. "I got it! Return to the scene of the crime."

"Crime? What crime? I said nothing about a crime," Matt said. *At least I hope there's not one.*

"No, no. Return to where you last met this guy—"

"Trent."

"Yeah, Trent. You know, like going back to the place you remember you had your keys when you lose them,"

Hunter said. "You told me you met him when you were backpacking?"

"Yeah. It happened about a day's hike from the trail-head," Matt answered. "Hang on a minute. You're not saying tramp all the way back to my campsite, do you?"

"No. How about the start of the trail?" Hunter asked. "Isn't it necessary for you outdoorsy types to get approved by Smokey Bear?"

Matt considered it, then brightened. "Yeah! A book by the ranger station! Backpackers and hikers have to sign in and out."

Hunter spread his hands out. "There's a start."

Matt nodded in agreement. "That it is."

"I'll drive."

Hunter borrowed his mother's SUV, about the size of a battleship. Matt shrank in his seat and leaned to the side, not only to be out of range but also to brace himself in case of sudden stops or swerves. Hunter's lousy driving skills meant he crazily concentrated on the traffic, not talking to Matt, or even listening to music.

However, this gave Matt time to think about the message he received from Trent. He held no doubt it was genuine, but how did Trent send it? He told Matt he had a five-foot range, and he certainly wasn't that close today. Also, the communication was directed specifically to him, and not a broadcast, either.

Did the game console get involved somehow? Did it serve as an amplifier? Or some kind of receiver like a radio?

Matt turned to his friend on the driver's side. "Hunter, can I turn on the radio?"

"I can't be distracted," Hunter said. "One more fender bender and the insurance company is going to demand my parents yank my license."

"Only for a second," Matt replied, "not loud."

Hunter nodded grudgingly.

Matt switched on the radio, kept the volume low, and sat back. He closed his eyes, making his mind blank. No messages appeared in his head. He got nothing at all. Perhaps the chips had to be of a certain complexity before he could pick them up.

He turned off the radio.

Trent's previous thought came to mind. And it was clear on one thing:

"He's in trouble," Matt said to himself.

Chapter Four

Hunter guided the SUV up the pass as Matt gazed through the windshield. He watched the scenery in a mesmerized trance.

The mountains surrounded the city, embracing it. They didn't look or feel real but condensed into two dimensions; he seemed to be viewing a huge painting. Row after row of mountain peaks marched into the distance, each range becoming bluer until the last row blended into the sky. Groves of pines and firs climbed up the slopes, like rambunctious children climbing into their grandfather's lap. Matt wondered if he should become a ranger, able to spend time in that glorious solitude.

The trail head was only forty-five minutes out of town and sat at the main entrance of a large national forest. Vehicles jammed the gravel parking lot and lined both sides of the road wherever they could fit, jostling to the entrance of the park itself. After finding one of the last open spots, Matt and Hunter climbed out of the SUV. Matt's nose twitched as he caught the scent of pine and fir and clean mountain air, mixed in with the smell of car exhaust and engine oil.

"Wow, this place is popular," Hunter said as looked around.

"Yeah. The main wilderness trail starts here, but there is also a campground, a convenience store, and a restaurant, and the whole thing sits right along a state highway. Like, the road is only two lanes wide, but it's one of the few ways across the mountains. Lots of drivers use this area as a rest stop," Matt said.

"No joke. The place looks like the mall parking lot the day after Christmas."

"It's also summer. Bunch of day trippers, too." Matt gestured with a hand. "The ranger station is over there."

The two strolled over to the small wooden building, painted standard Forest Service brown, topped with the standard green metal roof. Matt picked up a clipboard hanging from the wall below the open window. He flipped through the pages.

"Can I help you boys?" The ranger leaned out of the open window.

"We're checking if a friend of ours has come off the trail yet or not," Hunter answered. "We're supposed to meet him here to give him a ride home."

"Here he is," Matt muttered as he tapped a signature on the page. "But that can't be right."

"What can't be right?" The ranger seemed a little putout Matt was questioning his paperwork.

Hunter spoke up, "We agreed to drive our friend to town as I said. He had no other way back, and we haven't found him yet. Perhaps you remember him?"

"Listen, sonny, I see a bunch of people," started the ranger in exasperation.

"He came through about 7:00 this morning, according to this," Matt said. "He's as tall as I am and has blonde hair and blue eyes. Well-built. Could have been wearing a black tee-shirt ..."

"It's very important we find out," Hunter added with well-faked absolute sincerity. He threw a glance toward Matt. "His brother here is worried about him."

The ranger smiled after he thought about it. "Yes, yes, I recall your brother. He came through as I opened up. He asked if our restaurant served an excellent breakfast, and I said it was the best for miles around!" He chuckled. "Of course, there's only one around here for miles!" He roared at his joke.

Matt gave a weak smile while Hunter guffawed along. *He is good*, Matt thought.

"So, did he have that excellent breakfast?" Hunter probed with a grin as if still tickled by the ranger's jest.

"Must have. I went for a cup of coffee at the restaurant and saw him leaving. He was with two other fellas. Big guys on either side of him. All three got in the other guys' car."

"What kind of car was it?" Matt asked.

"We may know whose it is ... who took him back to town," Hunter put in.

"Oh, they drove a nice German sports number. Sleek. Black. I've always wanted one of those," the ranger sighed. "Well, anyway, I guess somebody else picked him up. No need to worry."

"But—" Matt started.

Hunter interrupted with a slap on Matt's back, "That sounds like old Trent, all right. Tells us one thing and does another." He laughed, tapped his temple with an index finger, and made a face. "You know how blondes are ... not the sharpest knives in the drawer." He pulled Matt away from the ranger station and waved with his free hand. "Thank you for your help, sir. He's probably home now, wondering where we are."

Matt disengaged from Hunter's grasp when they reached the parking lot. "This doesn't make sense. Trent was scared of them."

"But Ranger Rick there said …"

Matt ignored the comment. "He didn't get into the car himself. They got him."

"They got him? What, like, snatched him … a kidnapping? Who are they? Are we going into full conspiracy mode now?"

Matt gave an irritated growl and shrugged as he gazed over the parking lot. "I don't know. You're the mystery book fan. Think of something." He snapped his fingers. "Hang on. Trent probably drove here, but he left with those other guys, whether he wanted to or not. Either way, his car should still be here. That may be a start."

"Yeah!" Hunter brightened and started moving toward the lot. "What did he drive?"

Matt stopped. "No idea."

"Well, that makes things a little difficult." Hunter waved at the crowded parking. "Pick a car, any car."

Matt thought for a second. "Hey, hold on, hold on. He said he came from a cattle ranch in the high desert—"

"—So we'll check the plates!" Hunter finished. He gestured to the nearest car's license. "Vermont. Not exactly desert-like. Time for the license plate game!" He pointed. "I'll take that row."

"I'll keep on this lane," Matt said. "Don't look like you're casing a car to steal some wheels."

Hunter held up a finger. "Do not worry. I shall be the soul of discretion. Remember, sir, I am an actor." He moved off to the nearest vehicle.

Matt sauntered down his line of cars, trying to appear as though he was just stretching his legs after a long drive. He cast sidelong glances at the car's plates.

Local ... local ... Oregon ... Florida ... local ... Arizona ...

Matt stopped. Arizona. Desert, cattle ranch, that could be it, he thought. Then he checked out the car: a late-model Japanese luxury car. Matt shook his head. He doubted Trent drove one of those.

He continued down the line of cars.

Local ... local ... local ...

He halted again, this time by an older, beat-up red pickup truck.

"Nevada plate," he mumbled to himself. He noticed something on the corner of the rear bumper: a university student parking sticker from the spring semester. Trent said he had attended college for a while. He turned toward Hunter, who was already on the next aisle. "Hunter! Here!"

Matt moved to the driver's side. The truck was dusty like it had been sitting outside for a few days. He peered into the window and spotted Trent's backpack on the passenger side floor, a black tee-shirt thrown over the back of the seat. He tried the door. Locked.

"Of course," he groaned to himself and yanked on the handle again with an angry grunt. "He dropped off his pack, changed his shirt, then went to the restaurant to eat."

"What did you do, Joe, lock the keys inside, you idiot?"

Matt turned toward Hunter's voice. Hunter stood by the tailgate, hands planted on his hips. He jerked his head slightly at a couple walking behind him. The man was watching them with suspicion as he pulled his keyring from his pocket.

Matt shrugged sheepishly. "Like you've never done something like that, Frank."

"Not in this truck, I haven't, you moron," Hunter said. "And that's the truth. Now what?"

"Call the auto club?" Matt responded.

"Our phones are inside the cab, too, dummy!" Hunter exploded.

The couple walking behind Hunter stopped. The man spoke, "Do you two guys need help? I can use my phone to call ..."

Hunter momentarily was at a loss for words. "Uh ..."

The key is under the bed liner. Now I understand what Trent meant!

Matt walked toward the rear of the truck. "No worries. I have a spare."

"You do?" Hunter barely contained his surprise.

"Yes, I do." Matt shooed Hunter back a few steps and lowered the tailgate. He hoped Trent was righthanded and logically would have slipped an extra key underneath that edge of the bed liner. Matt reached under the heavy plastic and released an inward sigh of relief. He extracted the key, with a black rubber grip, from its hiding place. "Ta-dah! For my next trick!" Matt bowed and then gave Hunter a light shove. "Joe, Joe, Joe ..."

"I'm Frank."

"Frank, Frank, Frank, oh ye of little faith, brain of lame." He grinned and displayed the key to the man. "Thank you for your offer, sir. Everything is under control."

"Glad it worked out." The man smiled as he and the woman continued to their car.

"How did you ..." Hunter began.

"An inspired guess," Matt stepped to the driver's door and unlocked it. As he turned, he glanced out of the corner of his eye and noticed a black sports car with tinted windows enter the parking lot. It crawled along the far line of cars, stopping to let a van pull out of its spot. Even though vehicles filled the other spots, the sedan passed up the empty space and continued down the row. Matt took in a breath. The driver didn't want to park; he was searching for something ... like this truck.

"They're back," Matt said to Hunter in a singsong low voice, nodding toward the black sedan. He gave Hunter his keys. "Go back to your house, pick up my car, then meet me at my place in an hour."

Hunter hustled to his SUV as Matt climbed into the driver's seat of the truck. He inserted the key and twisted it. The engine kicked over, started, then stalled.

"Come on, baby, come on," Matt urged the pickup as he pumped the gas pedal.

He tried the ignition again. The engine caught, stumbled, and died. The truck started when he turned the key a third time. He shifted into reverse, pulled out of the space as fast as he dared, and hoped the truck wouldn't stall. He glanced over his shoulder.

What he saw was the black sedan turning at the end of the row and speeding up, heading for Matt. Hunter's SUV backed out in front of it and brought the car to an abrupt stop, narrowly avoiding a collision. The drivers of both vehicles honked, accompanied by hurled curses, Hunter's sounding like he came from the Bronx.

Matt threw his head back and laughed, then hit the gas again. Gravel and dust spewed from the rear wheels as he headed for the parking lot exit. He swerved left on the narrow highway, the tires squealing in protest. He steered the truck up the steep road in the direction of the pass.

The engine roared as if grinding coffee beans as Matt pushed his foot down on the gas pedal and shifted into a lower gear. The pickup heaved its bulk up the hill, laboring as it went. Its speed was still too slow to outrun that sedan. He almost reached the summit when he glanced in his rear-view mirror: the black car had exited the parking lot and was gaining on him.

The truck crested the pass and started descending the steeply angled downhill road, one edge tight against the mountain, the other at the lip of a precipitous drop into a deep canyon, lined with a flimsy guardrail that hardly warranted the name. Here and there, roads sloped into the side canyons.

Matt shifted into a higher gear but kept his foot on the gas, hoping gravity would give him a boost of speed. He hurtled down the pavement toward town, hugging the curves as he desperately clutched the wheel, willing the truck to ignore its determined desire to lose grip on the asphalt and slide off the cliff. The black car zoomed up behind Matt, filling the rear-view mirror. The sedan jumped forward, hitting his bumper, the impact jerking him into the steering wheel.

Matt's pursuer pulled out, as though to pass, but turned back in, its right front bumper striking the truck's left rear one. Matt spun the wheel as the pickup fishtailed, tires screaming, and managed not to go into a skid. The black car moved out to try a second time, but suddenly returned behind Matt and slowed.

A huge RV, about the size of a Greyhound bus, crawled uphill in the opposite lane. It seemed the sedan's driver wanted no witnesses to running Matt into a ditch.

Matt reached a level section of the highway at the base of the mountain. As soon as the RV disappeared around a bend in the road, the black car shot ahead and drove up behind Matt. There were no other vehicles in sight. The sedan again drew up next to the truck's left rear bumper and clipped it, successful this time in sending Matt into a sickening full circle spin like a cheap carnival ride before coming to a stop straddling the double yellow line. The car zoomed past him and pulled over to the side of the pavement and made a U-turn, churning up a rooster tail of dust and pebbles as it headed back toward him.

"I am so done with you!" Matt stomped on the truck's accelerator, laying a patch of rubber as he tore off down the blacktop, aiming the truck at the fancy hood ornament on the black sedan. He didn't know what he was going to do next, but one thing was certain: he had now had enough of playing bumper cars. Time to up the game with this clown to chicken.

The driver of the sports car gripped the wheel, his face a mask of concentration as he drove, the passenger's just as grim, his hands braced against the dash. Matt drew closer to the sedan until the two seemed to be inches apart. Then Matt stomped on the brakes and slid the truck into a sharp left turn. The car's front bumper thumped against his rear fender. The pickup swerved, and the sedan appeared to lose control for a second but kept going straight. Matt swung the truck back on the asphalt, the tires screeching in pain. He floored the accelerator again, the engine roaring like it was about to explode, and skidded around a tight, blind curve.

Another roadway entered from one side ahead. A big rig was halfway through, making a left turn into Matt's lane, the cab crossing the center yellow line. Matt yanked on the steering wheel. He shot past the front of the tractor-trailer in time to avoid a collision at the last second. The semi angrily blasted its horn and slammed on its brakes, blue acrid smoke bellowing from the wheels. Another large truck was traveling in the opposite direction. It braked to prevent smashing into the other big rig, a second air horn ripping through the air.

Matt checked his mirror. No sign of the other car. His traffic jam caused by dodging the big rig blocked both lanes, and his pursuers must be held up on the other side. He took a right on a bumpy, poorly maintained blacktop road branching off the highway. He pulled behind some trees and waited. In a few minutes, he peered through the leaves as the black automobile raced by, not noticing him.

Matt switched off the engine and leaned his forehead on the wheel. He breathed heavily, lightheaded from the adrenaline pumping through his veins. Sitting back in his seat, he held up his hands. They shook. He willed them to stop, but they just kept jittering. He closed his eyes and took a few deep breaths. When he opened them again, the dancing had subsided.

Those guys in the other car played rough. But like Hunter had asked, who were 'they'? From *the* government, or *a* government? A corporation? A cult? Other telepaths who didn't want their secret to get out? All he understood was that they were involved with Trent's disappearance.

He needed to find out more about the two goons in the black sedan, what they were doing, and what they wanted. They had grabbed Trent—he was sure about that—but they were also after this truck. Why?

Since he sat in the cab, he might as well start there. He glanced around the interior; nothing appeared out of the ordinary. It was simply the inside of a working ranch pickup. His eyes fell on the backpack. It was the most likely spot to begin to look, so he yanked the pack onto the passenger seat, unzipped it, and dug through the contents. He dumped to the floor the expected items carried by any backpacker but found nothing unusual. So much for a quick answer. He needed to get the truck home and make a thorough search, perhaps finding what the guys in the other car wanted.

That brought Matt back to his first question: Who are *They*? He capitalized the pronoun in his mind like it was a name or a title.

He sat in the truck, trying to tease some loose ends out of the knot. His phone buzzed, causing him to jump. Taking it out of his pocket, he checked the screen.

It was a text from Hunter: "Whr r u?"

Matt didn't realize he'd been parked for so long. He tapped a reply: "Held up in traffic. B there soon."

He tossed his mobile on the passenger seat, started the engine, and backed up. Stopping when he reached the highway, he glanced both ways, nervously wondering if that sedan would be lurking for him out there like a black widow spider. He took a deep breath and shook his head. No, They most likely had given up. They. Who were They?

Matt had no way of knowing, but he had the feeling he was about to find out.

Chapter Five

MATT KEPT CHECKING HIS rear-view mirror compulsively on the drive back to his house. Any black car he spotted triggered a sharp intake of breath until he could assure himself it was not the one he feared. At last, he turned on his street and a long, relieved sigh escaped him. Another quick glance behind him confirmed the sedan hadn't picked up his tracks again. He pulled into his driveway, next to his own car. Hunter sat in the driver's seat.

"Hit the garage door switch, will you?" Matt called out.

The door rumbled open, and Matt eased the red truck inside. He climbed out and waited for Hunter to join him before pushing the close button on the wall. The door rolled shut, rattling and squeaking, the garage growing darker.

"What traffic slowed you down?" Hunter asked as Matt switched on the fluorescent lights. "I checked for any road delays on my phone."

"There almost was an accident. Me," Matt described his encounter with the black car.

Hunter's eyes grew wide, and the round lenses of his glasses magnified them owl sized. He took a deep breath. "Dude, this is serious ...You need to call the cops."

"So what do I tell them?" Matt shrugged. "I got mixed up in a case of road rage. A black sports car tried to run me off the highway. End of report."

"Don't you know the make? It may be the one that you think Trent was forced into," Hunter said.

"Dude, I'm not a car nut. I saw some kind of hood ornament," Matt recalled.

"Star shaped?"

"I think so ... yeah, yeah, like a star in a circle."

"It's a Mercedes Benz," Hunter said. "What about the license number?"

"I was a little too busy to notice."

"The ranger said he thought he saw a German sports car driven by those guys with Trent. Mercedes is a German make. See? That's more information. Tell the cops—"

"Look, some crazy dude in a black Mercedes comes after me. I call the cops," Matt mimed holding a phone, "Do I know the model? No. Did I catch a license plate number? Sorry. Can I describe the driver? Uh, no. Well, thank you for your report, sir. Have a nice day." He pretended to hang up and shrugged.

"What about Trent? They can't ignore a kidnapping," Hunter persisted.

"Same deal. I talked with him for about ten minutes, tops, then I get like a premonition he needs help," Matt said. "Do you think the cops will believe me?"

"But you said those guys forced Trent into that car," Hunter pressed.

"The ranger told us Trent got into a car with two other guys. He didn't sound like they made Trent go with them."

"But you said Trent didn't get in willingly," Hunter argued.

"I still don't think he did, but the ranger didn't see it that way, and that's what he would tell the cops." Matt sighed. "So, we're at the end of the road with the men in blue. At least for now." He didn't need to be in range to realize Hunter was frightened. Frankly, he was too. He turned to face his friend. "I'm in this deep. I didn't mean to suck you in. I appreciate you hanging with me this far ... but I've got to keep going. I have to. You can bail."

Hunter was quiet for a moment, then stared Matt in the eye. "My first appearance on stage, I was scared to death. So frightened I puked before I went on. People called me 'shy Hunter', but that wasn't who I was. I knew that. After that first show ... no, after the second time ... no, make that the third performance ... I got used to being in front of an audience and felt I could control my nerves. And I did. I decided that fear wouldn't rule me. Ever."

Matt smiled. "You're so sick." He paced slowly as he worked things out. "If just taking Trent solved their 'issue,'" he tossed air quotes around the last word, "why go after me or the pickup?"

"To make the package pretty? Tie up loose ends?" Hunter suggested. "If they left the truck in the parking lot, somebody would tag it abandoned eventually. That could kick off an investigation."

"That's one reason. Or this group ... gang ... whoever ... is afraid of what they think I know or something I have." Matt tapped a fender. "Or something hidden in this truck."

"Then it's time to find out." Hunter clapped his hands like a stage manager. "Places, please, places!" He stalked to the truck. "Now, let's plumb the depths of this mysterious vehicle! The Hardy Boys in *The Secret of the Battered Pickup*." He hummed a musical sting.

Matt walked up behind Hunter. "I already checked the backpack. I found nothing."

Hunter threw off a sarcastic, theatrical laugh, rolled up his sleeves, and made a wild flourish with his hands. "And you call that a search? Stand back, rank amateur!"

The two boys tore into the pickup, looking in every nook and cranny. While Hunter was searching under the truck, Matt yanked off the passenger seat cushion, and he hit pay dirt: the neuro-pulsomic-jammer. He grasped the device and pulled it out.

He turned it over in his hand, examining the case for any markings at all. Nothing. A black box with a single switch on the side. He almost flipped it on, but stopped at the last moment, remembering Trent's warning about 'they can track it'. No need to send up a flare. Trent all but admitted he stole the device, so those guys in the other car may want the gizmo back, and bad.

He opened his mouth to tell Hunter, then thought better of it. No sense in spreading the information about the jammer around. It may be safer for Hunter not to know about it and also prevent questions to Matt about its function. He slipped the apparatus into this pocket just as Hunter appeared at the driver's door, his face and fingers spotted with dirt and grease. Matt had to laugh. His friend looked like a mechanic.

"Nothing under the frame." Hunter sat in the driver's seat and ran his hands behind the dash. "Wait! I found something!"

Matt was surprised. He figured the jammer was the only secret the truck contained.

"It was under the lip." Hunter held up a small USB drive. "Unusual place to store this."

"It sure is, and there is only one thing to do with it!" Matt snatched the stick and started up to his room, taking two stairs at a time. He booted his laptop. A wave of messages swamped his brain like a storm surge.

/usr/libexec/gdm-x-session[1585]: (WW) modeset(0): hotplug event: connector 105's link-state is BAD, tried resetting the current mode. You may be left with a black screen if this fails ...

/usr/libexec/gdm-x-session[1585]: (WW) modeset(0): hotplug event: connector 105's link-state is BAD, tried resetting the current mode. You may be left with a black screen if this fails ...

It took a second for Matt to realize he must be reading the computer's startup sequence commands, just like he had picked up the 'thoughts' of the game console. He shoved himself back from his desk to lessen the onslaught. "This is going to get real old real fast," he said under his breath. He sensed Hunter coming up behind him, but he waited until he heard Hunter speak.

"Afraid of the gamma radiation from the screen or something?" Hunter asked.

Matt swiveled toward Hunter and grinned. "Yeah. The electromagnetic waves may stop me from having kids."

Hunter imitated a robotic voice and waved his arms up and down stiffly. "Ster-il-ize ... Ster-il-ize."

The computer completed booting, and Matt rolled his chair back to his desk. The CPU kept reporting it was waiting for a command, almost as annoying as a buzzing gnat. Matt pushed the message to the rear of his mind and inserted the USB drive. A single icon appeared on the screen.

"Only one thing saved," Matt muttered. He deactivated the laptop's wi-fi. "In case something tries to call home. I had to reinstall the whole operating system after I got bit by a malware program in a game I downloaded last month." He double-clicked the icon.

The file opened, and a spreadsheet appeared.

Hunter read the heading. "'Subject: T.S. Age: 19 years 8 months.'"

"Trent Spencer," Matt confirmed.

"What do those mean, those row labels, going down the left?" Hunter pointed to the screen. "Alpha, beta, theta, delta, sigma, gamma, lambda?"

Matt leaned back in his chair, reducing the messages pinging his mind from the computer. "They're neural waves. At least, the first three are, so I guess the others are ditto."

"How do you know that, big brain?" Hunter crossed his arms.

"Amazingly, I stayed awake one day in science class." Matt didn't want to tell Hunter where he had learned the information. He leaned closer to examine the screen. "The columns are paired: the first named 'Hz' and the next 'Amp'. That pattern is repeated across the spreadsheet. Each pair has a heading."

"And those sets are labeled as 'Condition One', 'Condition Two', and so on," Hunter observed. "So what do the numbers mean in the cells?"

Matt stared at the figures and shrugged. "Findings of some type. Data."

"What kind?" Hunter pushed his glasses back up his nose.

"Oh, who knows?" Matt spat out in frustration. He threw up his hands. "The whole thing is meaningless. We don't know where the spreadsheet came from."

"Check the file properties tab. That may give us some clue." Hunter reached over Matt to access the trackpad. He opened the panel. "There ... here's the author's name: Ernst Richter."

"Ernst Richter," Matt repeated under his breath. "Time to ask the Google."

"Do a hard reboot," Hunter suggested. "Make sure you wipe the memory."

Matt nodded. "Good idea." He shut down the laptop, turned it off, removed the USB key, then started it again. Since Hunter was behind him, he couldn't push back from his desk. He gripped the chair arms as the computer's startup sequence marched through his brain one more time. He opened the browser. "Ernst Richter," he said to himself as he typed.

"Wow. Quite a number of hits." Hunter gestured to the search results.

"Most of the entries are about people who I doubt mess around with brain waves," Matt noted. "Here's an auto mechanic, a veterinarian, an actor ..."

"Never heard of him."

"Nobody has heard of you, either."

"Ouch! You cut me to the quick, sir," Hunter said. "Check out those, toward the bottom of the page. There, look! Ernst Richter, M.D."

"Yeah." Matt leaned closer to the screen. "It's an 'About the Faculty' page from the university website." He clicked on the link. "Here we go. Dr. Ernst Richter is an Associate Professor in the Department of Neurology." He skimmed the text. "Dr. Ernst Richter … German-born … specializes in sleep disorders … author of several books on the topic. He has an office in the Williamson Sleep Clinic." Matt sat back and tapped an index finger to his lips. "All right, some assembly required. Trent told me he went to college. The parking bumper sticker is for the university's spring term. He had a USB drive with data from Ernst Richter, who is a faculty member out there."

"And?"

"And we go talk to him." Matt closed the laptop and picked up the USB drive. "It's getting late. We need to hurry."

"What are we going to say?" Hunter asked.

Matt stood and moved out of range of Hunter. He needed to think without interfering outside thoughts. "I'll ask about his research."

"And if he asks why you're interested?"

Matt considered that for a moment. "I'll tell him I'm thinking of going into that field and wanted to pick his brain."

"How do we work our way around ask about the drive?"

"We'll just tell him the truth." Matt scooped up his car keys and headed to the door. "We can say we found the

USB drive and wanted to make sure it goes back to the rightful owner."

"What if he asks where we found it?"

"My! We are full of questions today. We'll say we picked it up in the street," Matt decided after a pause. "I mean, it is close enough to what happened. Like. Sort of. Kind of. Well, good enough at least."

"How did we figure out it was his? The drive doesn't have any markings on it," Hunter said. "The only way to discover it belonged to him was to by doing what we did: opening the file and snooping."

"Good point," Matt agreed as they walked to his car. "I'll bet you'll think of something on the way."

"Here's something else. We return the USB drive, and Richter takes it and says thank you very much, then what?" Hunter continued, "We're no further along than now."

"Maybe I can pick something up," Matt said, although he didn't tell Hunter how he could do that by telepathy.

"How?"

"Through questions, maybe something in the office. Perhaps I can drop Trent's name and see if there is a reaction," Matt hedged.

Hunter held up his hands. "I need to clean up first."

"You know where the bathroom is," Matt said. "I'll meet you in the garage."

When he reached there, he pulled the jammer out of his pocket and scanned the walls until he spotted a shelf lined with coffee cans. He walked over and picked up each can, weighing the contents inside until he found one that felt about half full. Unsnapping the lid of the tin, he dumped the can's screws on a worktable, placed the device at the bottom, and covered it up as he loaded the can. Recapping it, he nestled the tin next to the others on the shelf.

He got in the driver's seat and waited for Hunter. As usual with his car, it took Hunter a couple of slams to latch the passenger door. Hunter leaned into Matt's range as he did this. Matt smiled. Hunter's actor brain was already at work, concocting a scenario. He backed out of the drive and headed to the college.

After what seemed like an endless driving tour through the university's parking lots, they found the one for visitors. They found a spot and climbed out of the car. From every direction, the campus spread over the hillside, a sprawling maze of stone, brick, asphalt, and glass. Each building had a different shape, decorated in various styles. Some were perfect, others a little worn with the facade cracked.

"The sleep center should be ..." Matt tilted his head toward a group of buildings.

Hunter grabbed his arm and guided him in the opposite direction. "Admissions is over here. I saw that on a sign by the lot entrance."

"Admissions? Why Admissions?"

"Because, my dear acting partner, here's the setup." Hunter pulled Matt nearer. "We are playing the roles of two prospective students considering applying to this august institution. Thus, we need some props to enhance our characterizations, say a few brochures from the Admissions office. As we wander around this picturesque edifice of higher education, said papers in hand, we 'find' the USB drive. And being the considerate young people we are, we decide to return it to the good doctor."

"Excellent!" Matt bowed. "Lead on, Macduck,"

"'Lay on, Macduff', is the actual line," Hunter corrected. "The character in Macbeth is Macduff, not Macduck."

"I bow to your superior knowledge," Matt inclined his head in tribute, "Quack, quack."

A large and modern building built of glass and steel housed the Admissions office: impressive on the exterior, simple on the interior. A long counter divided the space. On the far side stood a series of glass-walled cubicles where staff were busy at work on computers. Several comfortable, but industrial-looking chairs and couches grouped around low coffee tables took up the public side of the space, along with racks of literature.

They stepped up to the counter and a young woman with a name tag that read 'Amy' greeted them with professional courtesy. "Can I help you?"

"We were just looking around, touring your college," Hunter returned in the clipped, elite voice of a preparatory school student.

"I see." Amy's sprayed-on smile never wavered. "Do you know what your majors would be?"

"I rather fancy neurology," Hunter replied crisply.

"Oh, here's a brochure on our pre-med program," Amy enthusiastically handed over a pamphlet. "And your friend?"

Hunter waved one hand dismissively. "Merely the theatrical arts, I'm afraid."

Amy looked disappointed. "I'm sorry. I'm afraid I don't have any specific brochures on that major ..."

"No worries." Matt moved down the counter and filled in his name and address on a clipboard labeled 'More Info'.

Why not, he thought, *make his parents happy and take the initiative?*

"Well, let me give you some general information and admissions packets, and then if you have questions, feel free to ask." She handed them a stack of papers stapled together, along with a couple of pens. "Here's a map of the campus," she added, handing one to each of them.

"Thanks," Matt said as they turned to go.

"You're welcome," Amy called after them. "Oh, if you can return tomorrow, we're holding a campus-wide open house."

"How delightful!" Hunter sounded as if royalty had invited him to high tea.

They left just as a veritable platoon of other hopeful students, being shepherded by a stressed woman, piled into the office.

"That will make Amy happy." Hunter moved aside to let the group through the door. The two sat on a nearby bench. "This worked out better than I hoped!"

"How so?"

"A solution to the how did we find out the USB drive belonged to Dr. Richter problem." Hunter loosened one of the self-addressed envelope from his packet. He carefully peeled off the admissions office sticker from the address space and scrawled 'Richter' in its place with a pen. He stood. "Now to age it."

"Age it?"

"Yeah. You age props. That makes them look older and more authentic on stage. After all, our story is we found this on the ground, isn't it? It may have been in the dirt for a few days." He crumpled up the envelope, smoothed it out, then dropped it on the cement. He stomped on it, then shuffled it back and forth a few times. Picking it up, he carried it to a nearby drinking fountain and let some water splash on it. He presented the result of his work to Matt.

"There," Hunter proudly handed the now beaten-up envelope to Matt. "It looks like it has spent some time outside and got hit by the sprinklers. See? The water smeared the ink enough to at least make it out the name but disguise my scrawl. Richter is a doctor, isn't he? They always have lousy handwriting anyway. Now, forward to the sleep clinic!"

Checking their maps, they located a small brick building that looked as if it had been built in the early 1900s, two stories tall, with a row of windows at ground level, suggesting a full basement. It stood tucked behind some more modern constructions like it hadn't been given an invitation to the party. The curved roof line held gracefully to the shape of the building and a set of French doors that opened to a porch in front. A sign above the entrance announced to all who cared to read it that this was the Williamson Sleep Clinic.

Matt and Hunter went inside, the door shutting with a sharp but polite click behind them. Matt didn't know what he'd expected a sleep clinic to look like, but he imagined it would be more like a hospital than it appeared. The carpet was deep rose-colored and soft underfoot. A hush blanketed the whole place. Many chairs of various designs stood against one wall; several groups of seating huddled together in conversation nooks, some for two people and others for four or more. A soothing, and Matt suspected, scientifically determined correct shade of pale blue paint coated the walls. Framed abstract art prints, all in quiet pastels, blended in with the well-designed calm atmosphere of the place. Leaflets on sleep habits and disorders filled a small rack by the door.

Hunter pointed to the building directory. "Dr. Richter's office is room 116," he whispered. It was as though the clinic demanded it.

In keeping with the building's age, the doors were dark wood with pebbled, half-glass top sections. Number 116 hung slightly ajar. Hunter paused for a moment, giving his face the determined expression of an actor about to make an entrance on stage. He knocked softly on the door.

"Yes?" a voice called from inside.

"Dr. Richter?" Hunter swung open the door.

The office was small, with almost every inch of the wall taken up by overstuffed bookshelves. File cabinets occupied whatever space was left, with piles of folders on top. A young man with a receding chin sat behind an equally overloaded desk. He had black eyes that hid beneath a fringe of bangs and dirty-blonde hair.

"Dr. Richter is in Germany on sabbatical," the man's deep voice sounded like it was shredding metal. The words were polite, but the tone made it clear he did not appreciate the interruption. "I am his graduate assistant, Victor Sokolov. May I be of assistance?"

"Howdy. Sure pleased to make your acquaintance," Hunter spoke with the drawl of a Texas ranch boy's first visit to the big city. He and Matt walked up to the desk. "We're just here to look over your mighty fine school ..."

Sokolov's eyes flicked down to the brochures the boys carried and nodded.

"And we found something, and we thought it might belong to you ... er, Dr. Richter. If not, well, see, we all don't know where the lost and found department is." Hunter held out the envelope.

The young man took it and stood. He was quite tall. "It is at Security. If need be, I will take this ..." He felt the bulge in the envelope, tore open one end, and shook out the USB drive into a waiting hand. He glanced at the drive, then up at Matt and Hunter. "Where did you say you found this?" A hint of suspicion tinged his voice.

"Why, shoot," Hunter grinned and vaguely waved toward the campus, "just out there, in the flower bed, by the walk yonder."

Sokolov glanced at Matt, then his brow furrowed, as though he noticed something interesting. He smiled and stepped up to him, coming into Matt's range.

Matt recoiled. He had never encountered a mind like Sokolov's. The man was cold and calculating. His thoughts suggested he used people like objects, discarding them when they had served his purpose. He seemed like an ancient reptilian god with a dozen eyes, staring down at his sacrifice from a throne and mocking a lower form of life.

Quickly turning, Matt moved away from the graduate assistant to the nearest bookcase and began scanning titles. "Dr. Richter certainly writes a lot."

"He is very widely published." Sokolov's tone changed from irritation to friendly. He maneuvered to face Matt again.

"Has he done anything on lambda waves and extra-sensory perception or telepathy?" Matt edged away from the young man to scan more book titles.

"ESP and telepathy are fiction," Sokolov declared. "Where did you hear that, particularly about the lambda waves?"

"Trent said something about it," Matt responded in a matter-of-fact tone.

"Trent?" Sokolov asked sharply.

"Why shoot, yeah, Mr. Trent," Hunter put in. "He's our science teacher. He's sick! We learn about ESP, telepathy, aliens ... oh, oh, and there's a government conspiracy to hide a UFO in Area 51 outside of Las Vegas—"

Sokolov's voice dripped with contempt. "How interesting."

Matt grabbed Hunter's arm and headed out the door, keeping his back to Sokolov. "Let's go, Joe. We still want to look over the stadium. Thanks for your time, Mr. Sokolov."

"Right, Frank. Yeah, thanks, you all!" Hunter called over his back.

Once they were in the hall, Hunter turned to Matt and opened his mouth. Matt shook his head in warning. The two said nothing until they walked a few feet from the building.

"What was all that about?" Hunter complained. "I thought you wanted information."

"He was getting suspicious," Matt said out of the corner of his mouth as he pulled out his map. "Careful. He's at the window, checking us out."

Hunter also consulted his map, then pointed in the distance. The two boys walked, taking in the sights until they were out of view of the sleep clinic.

"That Sokolov dude is mixed up in this. I'm almost positive," Matt said. "I saw the way he reacted to the USB drive and Trent's name. Nice save with the whole science teacher bit, by the way."

"I thought so."

They reached Matt's car and climbed in.

"What does it all mean?" Hunter latched his seat belt.

Matt shrugged. "I don't know yet. I need to turn it over in my brain."

He backed his car out of the space and drove to the exit. As he turned on the university's primary drive, he checked the rearview mirror. "Don't look back, dude, but I think we're being followed by a black sedan."

Chapter Six

"Is it the same car?" Hunter began to turn around in his seat.

"Don't look, don't look, don't look!" Matt commanded. He checked the rear-view mirror and nodded. "It's the same one, with some damage to the right front fender, where it tried to force me off the road."

"Do you think they'll try that now?" Hunter asked nervously.

Matt shook his head. "I don't think so. Too much traffic. I think they want to know where I live. How about the license? Can you see their plate?"

Hunter checked the passenger door mirror. "No. They're a couple of cars behind us."

"Drivers?"

"Two guys." Hunter turned to Matt. "What do we do?"

"I'll try to shake them off," Matt said.

"You're going to outrun them? In this skateboard?"

"No." Matt braked at a stoplight and glanced in the mirror. "I've played a bunch of auto theft and racing games. Let's see if I can do that in real life. Hang on."

The light flipped from red to green. Matt turned left on the next street, then left again, taking them in the same direction from where they had started.

Hunter had his eyes glued to the passenger-side mirror. "They just made the same turns. They're about four cars back." He looked out the windshield. "Matt, the light's red! We're going to get a ticket!"

"Good," Matt said. "I hope we will. Perhaps that'll slow them down."

Matt ran the stop light, twisted the wheel, and cut across the road, streaking in front of a bus heading in the opposing lane. He turned at the next corner and traveled down a narrow alley that passed behind the police station.

"There's the—" Hunger began.

Matt made another turn to go back to their original street. He drove in an aimless pattern for another fifteen minutes until he had made sure the black sedan wasn't behind him.

"That should do it. Simple." Matt pulled up in front of Hunter's house. "Now, let them figure out where I went."

"Well, thank you for a lovely time," Hunter said as though he was on his first date. "It has been something to remember. We need to do it again sometime."

Matt chuckled, then became serious. "Dude, thanks for your help. You're bussin'."

"Anytime, Joe, anytime." Hunter grinned. "The Hardy Boys always get their man. Or is that the Mounties?" They fist-bumped. "What's next?"

"I don't know, I just don't know." Matt shook his head, thinking for a second. "Those dudes in the black Mercedes must be connected with the Sleep Clinic somehow. Like, we just visit there, and Bam! We have a tail. I'll dig into that Sokolov guy more. See what I can find online. I'll text you what I find."

"I need to play the dutiful son role and attend a wedding-reception thing tomorrow in Springdale with my parents," Hunter said, "for some second cousin I've met like twice in my life. Your messages will be a most welcome break from the tedium."

Hunter climbed out of the car, and with a wave, walked up his front path to the porch. Matt waited until he got inside before checking his mirrors again. Not another car in sight.

He drove home, going over things in his mind. He had put none of the pieces together as he parked his car, lowered the garage door, and glanced at the searched truck, the pulled-out parts scattered around. When he stepped inside the kitchen, Sushi complained of not being fed dinner on time. He dumped some canned food into her bowl, scratching her head a bit as she ate. Microwaving a couple of hot dogs for himself, he ate standing at the counter.

He went back to the pickup and put it back together in an hour.

Nodding at a job well done, Matt returned to his room. He plopped down into his desk chair and leaned back, propping his head against the high back. He spun around in a circle once and stopped, swiveling from side to side while he worked through what he knew.

Matt's eyes fell on his laptop, and his memory flashed back to the first message he got from Trent. That seemed to come through Hunter's game console. If it happened once, why not again? The car radio may not have been the right kind of chip, but maybe his laptop ...

Matt switched on the computer, gritting his teeth as the boot commands marched through his brain. He pushed himself back from the screen, and after experimenting, determined that the electronic noise became more tolerable a foot away. As the desktop appeared, the flurry of messages from the laptop subsided, save for an occasional bleating from the CPU about its usage and temperature, and the trackpad patiently waiting for any activity.

One of his therapists taught Matt self-hypnosis to help him relax and ignore the voices. It didn't work, of course, but he wondered if it could be of use now.

He closed his eyes and leaned back in his chair. He gave himself the commands to reach the complete relaxation of a hypnotic state. His head dropped forward on his chest, his breathing deep and regular. He imagined the laptop in his mind's eye. As he watched, a wormhole on the screen opened, and he felt himself tugged through it. For a second, he couldn't decide if it was actually happening or just his imagination, but whichever it was, he couldn't stop his forward progress. He found himself in a void, full of nothingness, not bound to his chair, or even his body. The energy of the computer reached out to him, connecting with his mind, and flowing into his consciousness until he was no longer in his own world, but inside the computer.

His physical self faded, a mere afterthought, as his mind continued its journey. Swirls of colors appeared, the flickering pixels of life, shapes tumbling. He felt no sensation, no pressure, no warmth, no cold. He didn't know where he was—if indeed he was in a dimensional location at all. There was sound, but it was the sound of nothing, nothing running with empty wind, nothing crashing through the void. He called out in his mind.

Trent? Are you out there? Trent? It's Matt ...

The black velvet emptiness blotted up his thoughts.

Words appeared as if brought to life and given wings, like a swarm of bees in a hive. They overwhelmed him, a blizzard of letters swirling around. He concentrated, imagining a pair of hands shoving them in file folders. Once he corralled the words, he selected a blue folder and flipped it open.

Int gdriver = DETECT;
int gmode;
int ch,is_ hit;
*int x=350,y=200;/*x,y coordinates*/*
*/*variables used to move around boxes*/*
q=0,j=320,k=400,r=0,m=800,n=200,p=600,o=300;

It was a program listing. He checked a red folder.

This notion of where economic power should lie ties into the greater internal geopolitical question that sparked the conflict. The secession of the South would mean, clearly, losing a sizeable portion of American territory.

His term paper for his American history class. Apparently, his telepathy skills extended to reading the mind of a hard drive.

The sound of a loud rumble upset everything. The contents of the folders flew open as if in a tornado. He felt pressure and sensation, and he was yanked backwards through the wormhole as though attached to an elastic band. His mind slammed back into his body.

Something bumped his chin, and he felt pinpricks on his legs. He opened his eyes. Sushi was on his lap, purring, kneading, and rubbing her head against Matt's chin. He smiled as he scratched her head.

"Like, whoa." He ran his fingers through her fur as he stared at the laptop, transfixed. Was he actually inside it, or was it only a figment of his imagination? He didn't know how to program but had read lines of computer code. He'd seen the paper he had written last year with perfect clarity. His memory had merged with the computer, and he could read its mind. His telepathy gave him an unimaginable connection to a world beyond his own and enabled him to cross into a new universe, yet he feared what would happen if he fully embraced it. "My alternative career path: Computer Whisperer. Problem with your computer? Let me read its mind."

Despite the weird experience, though, it failed. It didn't duplicate what had happened with Hunter's game console. Maybe Matt's original idea was correct. To get a message, it required something like a radio. One person needed to be on a sending set and the other one on a receiver simultaneously. That meant Matt had to return to more mundane methods to find Trent. The only clue he had was the Sleep Clinic.

Trent attended the university and somehow become involved with the Sleep Clinic. Perhaps they treated him. Matt shook his head. The spreadsheet labeled 'T.S.' as 'Subject,' not client or patient. He assumed 'T.S.' stood for 'Trent Spencer'. It may be the same as 'Tom Smith' though.

"That can't be right," Matt said to himself.

How did Trent possess another person's records? Were they sent to him? Given to him? Did he also steal them along with the device? And why hide the USB drive in the truck, as though it contained the secret launch codes for nuclear missiles?

Matt shifted in his chair to get more comfortable. The initials, along with the labels 'subject' and 'conditions,' suggested an experiment. Trent was the only 'subject' listed and not numbered. That could mean he was most likely the lone member of the experimental group. Why would he be in a test involving brain waves? Only one reason came to mind.

"Telepathy," Matt said out loud.

It had to be. Despite Sokolov's assertion that things like telepathy and ESP were false, either he or Richter must have discovered Trent's abilities and persuaded him to take part in a study. One result could have led to the development of the neuro-pulsomic-jammer. Then something bad could have happened during the experiment, with Richter, Sokolov, and Trent having a falling out of some sort. Trent stole the jammer and his experimental file and fled the university. He must have known he was being pursued by Richter and Sokolov's men. They had to employ the guys in the black sedan. Trent must have tried to lose them in the wilderness, so he hiked into the forest where he met Matt.

Matt leaned forward, excited. He tapped his fingers against the desk. "That's it, that's it."

That's why Trent was so nervous; he was worried about his pursuers. He said the jammer could be tracked, so when he turned it on to surprise Matt, Sokolov, and Richter most likely received a signal of its approximate location. Trent probably believed he had stayed in the wilderness long enough to throw off his followers, but he was wrong. When he came off the trail, the Black Sedan Boys had to have taken him.

Then Matt hit a brick wall. What next? Where did they take him? He swore.

Matt became antsy. He couldn't just sit here, so he checked the time. Night classes would continue for another hour. Perhaps he should pay a return visit to the Williamson building.

Dumping Sushi off his lap, he jogged to his car and drove back to the campus. It was quieter at night, the lights throwing yellow pools on the sidewalks. Classes were finished for the evening. Students toting backpacks headed for the parking lots as cars started and headlights flicked on. Matt made his way to the clinic. The office windows were dark, and only the corridors were lit. He went inside, softly closing the door behind him.

The second floor and basement stairs stood to his right. He started downstairs and planned to work his way up. He followed the steps down.

The hallway was empty; perhaps he was alone in the building. The faint buzz of the fluorescent lights, and the padding of his own footsteps as they hit the linoleum floor, were the only sounds. A sign posted at the bottom of the stairs admonished: QUIET PLEASE. SLEEP STUDIES IN PROGRESS.

The restrooms were on the left wall. Doors lined the right side of the corridor in groups of three. The first door he passed was marked 'Sleep Lab 1', the next one was 'Control Room', and just beyond was 'Sleep Lab 2 Soundproofed'. The next set of rooms was the same, but one number higher. An additional notice posted below 'Sleep Lab 4 Soundproofed' read 'Do Not Disturb. Experiment in Progress'.

The noise of something hitting the wall inside the control room and the twist of the doorknob sent Matt darting across to the men's restroom. He leaned against the door to urge the pneumatic closer to shut faster. The door across the hall opened.

"The building should be vacant now," a voice said. "Check the alarm."

"Right, right, okay," another voice answered.

"Get me some coffee, too," a third voice ordered.

Footsteps faded away as they climbed the stairs. Thin, scratchy words floated over what sounded like a small speaker. "Please ... let me sleep ... I'm so tired ..."

Matt tensed as an icy shiver ran through him. The voice sounded like Trent. He cracked the restroom door open. The control room door was ajar.

Taking a deep breath, Matt squeezed between the bathroom door and frame, sliding down with his back against the wall. He stopped opposite the control room and cautiously peeked in.

Matt saw a part of a small space dominated by a console. It was dark, the only light coming from two monitors. One showed the green repeated pulses of what could be a heartbeat. The other displayed an image of Trent, stripped to the waist. His wrists were tied together and suspended from the ceiling. He wore headphones, and two electrodes trailed wires from his chest. A bright light bathed him.

"I can permit sleep, but only after you provide the correct information." Sokolov's tall figure materialized out of the darkness as he leaned forward on the console, fiddling with a pen held in one hand, the monitors throwing a cool illumination on his pale face. The blackness left half his face in shadow, giving him the pallor of the living dead.

"I already told you everything ... I must sleep ..." Trent's eyes closed, and his head fell forward.

Loud clanging of bells sounded. Trent's eyes opened and his head snapped back. He groaned. The bells stopped. "No ... please ... no more ... I'm so tired ..."

"How did those kids get the drive?" Sokolov tapped the pen on the console impatiently. "What do they know?"

"Kids? Who ... in the truck ... I don't know ... I can't think ..." Trent's voice trailed off.

The bells rang again, and he cried out.

"We'll just go over it again. How did they get the truck?" Sokolov leaned back, swallowed by the shadows again.

"Spare key ... I told him where ... Stop ..." Trent could barely form words, "... please ... he knows nothing about you ... please, have mercy ... let me sleep."

"He has a powerful will," Sokolov observed with some irritation.

Another man growled from the darkness. "Ah, let me work him over. I'll end his powerful will."

"No," Sokolov's reply was tart. "He's too valuable."

An angry, wordless grumble from the other man came in response.

Time to leave the clinic building and call the cops, Matt decided, but that meant he had to slip unseen past the open door. He took a breath and moved. His tennis shoe sole squeaked against the floor.

"What's that?" Sokolov asked. "Somebody may be in the hall. Check."

There was a protesting groan and swish of a chair swiveling. Footsteps shuffled down the stairs at the same time, trapping Matt in the middle. He fled back to the restroom.

"Oh, it's only you," the gruff-voiced man said.

"Who else?" another man asked.

"Is the alarm set and cameras working?" Sokolov demanded.

"Yes sir."

"Then, if anybody is in here, we'll catch him," Sokolov said. "I don't think we will be much longer."

A grunt was the reply. "Good. We can leave the door open. Too stuffy in there."

Matt could not let the so-called graduate assistant get away with this. The cops had to be involved now. The tiled bathroom walls echoed everything, so he moved to the very back corner where he could whisper without being overheard. At least he hoped so. He pulled out his phone.

"I need to pee," the gruff voice announced from across the hall.

Matt panicked. He frantically looked around the sterile room. There was no obvious place to hide. He ran to a stall and clambered on the toilet. He hunched forward to duck below the top of the partition, sliding his hands against the sides to steady himself. As he did so, he fumbled with his phone and it splashed into the bowl. He tried to reach for it, then froze.

The bathroom door opened, and footsteps walked over to the urinal. A zipper being pulled down, followed by the sound of a fire hose spurting, dragged on for minutes. The flow of liquid stopped, and a contented moan echoed off the tile walls. Another rasping zip resulted in more footsteps and the door opening and then closing with a soft hiss.

Matt climbed off the toilet and fished his phone out of the bowl, switching it off as fast as he could. His mobile was waterproof, but that didn't mean it could function like a submarine. He grabbed some toilet paper off the roll, drying the screen and the case as much as possible. So much for calling the cops, he thought. He dropped the tissue into the toilet and slipped the handset back into his pocket. He crept to the door and placed one ear on it.

"... risky to keep him here any longer. Get him to our other location," Sokolov was saying. "I'll clean up."

A scuffling sound came from the other side. Matt pulled the door open a sliver. Trent, his hands still bound, mumbling incoherent words, was being half supported and half dragged out of Sleep Lab 4 by two burly men built like NFL linebackers. The trio headed down the hall toward the stairs. Just as they turned the corner, Sokolov stepped out of the control room.

Matt shut the door. He leaned against the cold tile to wait until it was quiet again. He cracked the door and checked across the corridor. Sleep Lab 4 was open, and Sokolov remained in there, sounding like he was packing things up. He placed a small trash can outside the room, a torn tee-shirt draped over the edge and walked back inside. Matt could make out the letters 'Nev—' printed on the material. If Matt could retrieve it, that would be evidence that Trent had been here ...

Sokolov stepped out of the room. After throwing other things into the trash, he closed and then locked the lab door. He flipped over the 'Do Not Disturb' sign to 'Vacant'.

Picking up the basket, he returned to the control room. The sound of crumpling paper came from inside. So much for gathering evidence.

Matt knew it was too chancy to sneak past the open doorway. He glanced down the hall in the opposite direction of the stairway. An EXIT sign with an arrow pointing left glowed green at the far end. He flowed out of the bathroom and around the edge of the door like liquid, and crept down the hallway, his pace increasing as he neared the end. He rounded the corner. A pair of double doors, the glass upper half equipped with a wire screen to protect it from vandals, stood in front of him. They led to a short flight of steps to ground level. He reached out to push the bar to open the door.

It might as well have been a brick wall. Matt stopped so suddenly that he fell backwards on his rear. Plastered across each door was a sticker printed in red: EMERGENCY EXIT ONLY. ALARM WILL SOUND IF OPENED.

For a second, Matt considered blasting through anyway the doors anyway. He could be long gone before Sokolov followed. But then he noticed something else: a surveillance camera pointed down the steps at the exit. Even if he twisted his body so his face wouldn't be visible, he still wore the same clothes as he did this afternoon. If Sokolov saw the image, he could recognize Matt. Both Hunter and he carried brochures for the university; Amy of the Admissions Office might have noted Matt's interest on the sign-up clipboard and that he'd signed it. He might as well have provided turn-by-turn directions to his home.

Who cares! Matt angrily thought. *Let the police come and pick me up. I'll tell them everything!*

He stopped. What would he tell them? That he saw Victor Sokolov of the university's Williamson Sleep Clinic torturing Trent Spencer by depriving him of sleep because of his ability to read minds? Matt would have to convince the skeptical police about Trent's abilities without revealing his own. Sokolov was cleaning up at this moment, so there would be no trace left of Trent's presence. The word of a soon-to-be high school senior with a history of mental health treatment would be no match against that of a brilliant graduate assistant to a famed neurologist. Easy to figure out the winner of that little contest.

The hallway blacked out, leaving only the flickering fluorescent lamps of the outdoor security lamps to cast a sickly yellowish illumination on the floor, sliced up in a crosshatched pattern by the wire over the door windows. Matt crawled to the corner and peered down the hall. Sokolov's slender shadow, made grotesque by the first-floor lights, flitted along the stairwell wall like a ghost as he climbed upstairs, the carried trash bag resembling a severed head.

A soft beeping came from behind him. Matt turned toward it. A red light pulsated in sync with the tone on the alarm system controls next to the exit doors. The panel switched from ARMED to READY. From above, he heard the building's front door open and close, and the click of the lock echoing. The beeping stopped. The panel now read ARMED, blocky blue letters glowing in the dark.

"Brilliant. Absolutely brilliant," Matt muttered to himself.

He considered finding an unlocked window or something to let himself out but figured the building used motion detectors. His only option was to spend the night. He got as comfortable as possible and settled in.

Crouched in the dark, Matt's thoughts returned to his mistakes. He should have yanked the fire alarm. Maybe he should have burst into the Sleep Lab, freed Trent, and fought his way out. So many ways he could have handled this differently ... should have, should have, should have ... They surrounded him in the darkened corridor, pointing and jeering.

He pulled up his legs and hugged them, dropping his forehead to his knees.

It was going to be a long night.

Chapter Seven

AN ELECTRONIC CHIRP ROUSED Matt from an uneasy doze. For a second, he believed he was in his room, waking up in the morning for school, before he realized he still remained on the floor in the Sleep Clinic. Dawn light streamed into the corridor through the windows in the doors. He automatically reached for his phone to check the time, but stopped, not wanting to switch it on and fry the insides before they totally dried. The beep that woke him came from the alarm panel. The display now read READY.

Matt climbed to his feet, stiff from sitting on the linoleum all night. He stretched and crept to the corner to listen, straining to hear if anyone moved in the hallway. No noise. He peeked into the corridor. The coast was clear. He stepped out and looked both ways before heading toward the staircase. As he neared them, he heard movement on the floor above.

He froze, not knowing what to do. Continuing forward was his only option. He slipped off his shoes and crept up the steps as quietly as he could, his heart pounding in his chest. When he reached the top of the stairs, he peered through the banister railings, gripping them like jail bars.

A white A-frame sign reading 'Welcome to the Williamson Sleep Clinic' leaned against the wall. A folding table, loaded with Styrofoam coffee cups, stood by the front entrance. Voices and laughter drifted from an office down the corridor.

Matt smiled. He remembered the whole campus was holding an open house today. It's easy to leave now. All he needed to do was wait for a crowd of visitors, mingle in, then simply walk out with them. He spotted somebody stepping into the hallway, ducked behind the banister, and slipped back into the comparative safety of the men's restroom, pushing the door closed.

He sat on a toilet as he put on his shoes, almost giddy as the sound of more voices and footsteps floated down from upstairs. After maybe an hour and a half, he stepped into the basement corridor.

The sleep labs stood open, as were the control rooms. Groups of two or three people, prospective students, and their parents, he supposed, milled around. Curious, Matt entered the door of Sleep Lab 4.

It was small, painted a restful gray, containing a single twin-sized bed and a matching nightstand holding a dainty lamp. The lighting was low, just enough to see without straining the eyes. One wall contained a mirror, most likely one of those two-way jobs, allowing people in the control room to monitor the person under study. Matt looked up. Screwed into the ceiling over the bed was a metal ring, about in the area where Trent had been secured. He checked the floor. Small depressions, like from furniture casters, marked the carpet on the far side of the room, showing the bed may have been shifted there, possibly to allow for binding Trent, before being moved back to its original position afterwards.

Matt got a chill, as though the temperature had plunged ten degrees. Sokolov had walked into range. Matt turned around and instinctively stepped back. The graduate assistant stood behind him, one hand on the doorknob.

"Please don't close the door," Matt said.

Sokolov's smile came out of the freezer. "Why, it is almost as though you could read my mind."

Matt's returned smile was just as cold. "You told me yesterday that ESP and telepathy were fiction."

Sokolov shrugged and began to swing the door shut.

"Do not close that door," Matt repeated firmly, "or that pretty little lamp goes through that big expensive mirror. And I yell as loudly as I can."

"Your supposition is incorrect. Nevertheless ..." The young man bowed slightly and opened the door. "Are you claustrophobic?"

"No. I just don't like small spaces," Matt replied.

Two visitors poked their heads into the room. Sokolov oozed friendliness and interest as he spoke to Matt. "I'm glad you returned today. Are you interested in pursuing the study of sleep in college?"

"Let's say that certain aspects of brain function fascinate me," Matt responded.

"The human mind has many possibilities. A truly interesting subject. The often repeated statement that people only use ten percent of their brains is a myth, of course, but we still have a great deal to learn about its functions." The visitors withdrew their heads and went on down the corridor. Sokolov continued, "Is your friend, Trent was it, here with you today?"

Matt didn't have to read Sokolov's mind to pick up on that rather obvious ploy. "Mr. Trent is my science teacher."

"Oh, yes, that's right, of course. UFOs, aliens, and such," Sokolov waved a hand in dismissal, "You must forgive me. I'm afraid I've forgotten your names."

"No worries. We didn't tell you," Matt said.

"Oh, and ..." Sokolov waited expectantly.

A movement of Sokolov's hands caught Matt's attention. He glanced down and noticed Sokolov remove a hypodermic needle from his lab coat pocket. The two locked eyes. Matt read triumph in the young man's mind as his shoulders squared to take on his task. He took one step forward.

"Here are our labs," a perky female voice came from the other side of the mirror. "The control room is between the two rooms designed for testing. Here we have all our equipment to monitor a patient's sleep, such as an EEG, EKG, video and auditory monitoring."

Matt turned to the glass, waved his arms, and shouted. "Hey! Can you guys see me in there? Aren't these trick mirrors great?" He grabbed Sokolov by the shoulders and spun him to face the mirror. Sokolov shifted the hypodermic behind his back and smiled awkwardly at his reflection. "Can you see Mr. Suckaduck here, too?"

As laughter came from the control room, Matt moved behind Sokolov toward the door. As he passed, he pushed the syringe in Sokolov's hand into his rear cheek and pressed the plunger. Sokolov took a sharp breath, but Matt's telepathy gave him a glimpse of Sokolov's discomfort, and that made him happy.

"Oh, pardon me," Matt said with mock sweetness, "that was clumsy of me."

He quickly exited the Sleep Clinic, wondering exactly what he had injected Sokolov with; or, rather, what Sokolov intended to inject into him. One thing was for certain: the hypo didn't hold a vitamin shot.

The campus bustled in a flurry of activity, with visitors wandering through the grounds like aimless ants. Matt mixed in with the crowd, careful to make sure nobody was on his tail before he headed for his car.

Matt kept an eye on the road behind him as he drove home, on the lookout for any cars that might be trailing him. He worried about Trent and what could have happened to him after last night, but remembered Sokolov called Trent 'valuable', so he probably wouldn't be killed. But that still left room for a lot of other unpleasant possibilities, as he had witnessed. The Sleep Clinic's involvement in Trent's disappearance couldn't be more obvious.

When he reached home, the one thing Matt didn't need to worry about was coming up with a story to tell his parents why he was gone all night, since they were floating somewhere on the Mediterranean. Neither did he have to worry about Sushi. The cat had tipped over her dry food and was happily munching on the contents, her rear end projecting out of the open top of the bag. Matt stroked her, then grabbed a small casserole dish from the cabinet. He placed his phone in it, then dumped some rice on top. Taking the dish to his room, he put it on the nightstand.

A glance out the window showed no traffic on the street, nor any strangers lurking under the elm trees. Matt's body felt heavy. He'd dozed a little last night, but he still was exhausted. He undressed to his boxers, then gratefully climbed into bed.

Matt fell asleep almost immediately.

He awoke hours later with the sensation of something clamped over his mouth. To his shock, he found eyes staring back at him through a black ski mask. At first, Matt struggled, but he stopped as the stranger's thoughts entered his mind: a feeling of love for the power of violence and waiting for any excuse to use it.

"Smart boy," the man growled through the mask. Matt recognized the voice: one he had heard last night at the Sleep Clinic. "Get out of bed."

Matt did so. A glance out the window told him it was probably late afternoon. Another man, this one wearing a dark blue ski mask, stood at the foot of the bed. He casually tossed a wide roll of adhesive tape up in the air and caught it like a baseball. He was as huge as the first man. These two must have carted Trent out of Sleep Lab 4.

"Sit at the desk," the first stranger commanded gruffly. "No noise."

Matt sat.

The second man professionally and efficiently taped Matt's wrists to the chair's arms and his ankles together. He finished by winding the tape several times around the middle part of Matt's torso, strapping his upper arms and back to the seat. He didn't look at Matt while he did all this, but focused on his work with a concentration that was almost fierce. A cold knot of fear twisted Matt's gut, greater than the discomfort at the adhesive that bound him.

After completing his job with the tape, the goon in the blue ski mask lowered the window blinds, dimming the light in the bedroom until it was like twilight. Outside, the high-pitched laughter of children playing and the rhythmic slap-slap-slap of a lawn sprinkler came in stark contrast to the quiet tension filling the air in the room.

The mysterious figure that had spoken stood in front of Matt was taking out a pair of rubber gloves from his pocket and carefully fitting them onto his large hands. Each glove was pulled and stretched over his fingers, the sound of them snapping in place at his wrists ominous in the quiet room. His voice was threatening and his gaze as cold and hard as steel.

"We'll start with the simple questions."

The second man stepped next to the first, holding one of Matt's leather belts. He handed it to the other man, who doubled the belt and snapped it. The sound was sharp and sudden, like a gunshot in the silence. Matt thought he detected the corners of the man's mouth turned up under the ski mask in a satisfied smirk of anticipation.

Matt flinched as the man snapped the belt again and leaned in.

He almost whispered, "How did you and your little pal lay your hands on that USB drive?" He bent close enough to Matt, and his thoughts came through like a bullhorn: *I'll make this punk talk*.

Matt's throat went dry. His tongue darted out to wet his lips. The man, clearly proud of his skills, would be disappointed if he couldn't show them off, Matt realized. They might not believe what he said without some 'persuasion' first. Matt would have to deal with this guy like his former therapists: make the goon think he did all the work and compliment him on his competence.

"We found the thing outside the—" Matt began.

The second man jammed his gloved hand over Matt's mouth. Matt tasted the talcum-powdered latex.

"We don't want to annoy the neighbors with any loud noises." The first man wielded the belt like a blackjack, lashing Matt multiple times. His screams became reduced to muffled gasps for air. The men stood back and waited for Matt to catch his breath.

"Our time is valuable. Don't waste it. Now where did you find it?" the first man said.

"I told you, outside—"

After a nod from the man in the black ski mask, the second clamped his hand over Matt's mouth. The first goon whipped Matt for several more seconds with the doubled-up belt, grunting with each blow, the leather biting into Matt's upper body, stinging heat spreading across his chest and shoulders. The men stepped away once more.

"Okay, okay. In the truck. It was hidden in the pickup," Matt groaned out.

"The red one parked in your garage?"

"Yes."

"How did you know where to return the drive?" the first goon demanded.

Matt shrugged. "Just a lucky guess, I suppose."

The first man looped the belt around Matt's neck, hanging on to an end. He handed the opposite one to the other man.

"Signal with one hand when you're ready to talk, smartass," the questioner ordered.

Matt extended both middle fingers. The leather tightened around his throat. He choked, struggling for air. His vision swam, and he felt like he was going to pass out. He thrashed, trying to escape, desperate to get air, but the tape held him down. Finally, he wiggled the fingers of his right hand. The men released the pressure.

"All right, all right, you win. Lay off, I get it. You're good." Matt swallowed and took a moment to collect himself. "I opened the file on my laptop, looked in the properties tab."

"Did you copy or save any files off the drive?" I first man asked.

"No."

The belt closed around his neck again.

"No, I said no, I didn't, no copies!" Matt croaked out.

"I just needed to make sure you were telling us the truth the first time." The first man leaned over Matt as the tension on his throat relaxed. The goon's thoughts radiated satisfaction at a job well done.

"How did you get the truck?" the second man asked.

Matt decided to risk saying whatever he wished, hoping the men believed he'd taken enough punishment to answer honestly. "I stole it. How do you think?" he retorted. "I met this guy on the trail. He whined that his family was rich, but his daddy wouldn't buy him a nice, new shiny pickup. So, I took his old one to, like, to help him out. Just to be friendly. That's me. I always help others. His daddy has to give him a new ride now."

The two men looked at each other. Matt didn't need to be in range to know what they thought. They nodded and grinned with approval, as though Matt were one of their own.

"And the drive? Why return it?" the goon in the black ski mask demanded.

"I thought I'd at least get a reward," Matt spat out bitterly.

That response was also met positively.

"Where is the key?" It wasn't really a question.

"Hey, I went to a lot of trouble—" Matt began. The belt slashed across his face, opening a cut below his left eye. "Top desk drawer."

"Sucks to be you, buttercup. You get no reward and no truck." The man rummaged through the drawer and pulled out the key. "This it?"

Matt nodded.

The second man tore off a long piece of tape, pressing it tightly over Matt's mouth and wrapping it around the back of his head. The two goons walked toward the bedroom door. They put their heads next to each other, talking softly, then laughed, pig-like grunts punctuated with a hiss escaping between their teeth.

They returned to Matt. One grabbed his ankles, while the other taped his legs together up to his knees, then they continued to tape Matt from his waist and upper arms to his neck, wrapping him like a mummy. The tightness of the adhesive made it difficult to breathe.

When they finished, they pulled out their phones and took selfies with Matt, laughing and posing. They whispered again. One man videoed the action, while the other grabbed hold of the chair and wheeled it out of the room. He propelled it down the hall like it was a toy car, making engine noise and tire squealing sounds. The man pushed the seat toward the staircase at the end of the hallway.

They're going to shove me down the stairs! Matt realized with horror and anger. He screamed and fought against his bonds. He tried putting his feet down as brakes, but only received a rug burn. The chair didn't slow down.

With one loud, muffled shriek of "No!", Matt's eyes snapped shut, and his whole body tensed up. The front wheels rolled off the floor and tilted down in empty space, suspended over the first step, and stopped, teetering on the edge.

An explosion of giggling, sounding like escaping steam, came from behind him. The chair jiggled back and forth a few times, inducing more laughter. The wheels were pulled back on the floor. One man kneeled, grabbed the base, and moved it so the front casters just perched on the lip of the top step. The two goons squeezed their bulk around Matt and started downstairs.

"Watch how you move, buttercup. Whatever you do, don't sneeze," one chortled. He jumped on the stairs. The chair vibrated, and Matt sucked in a breath.

The two intruders tromped down, laughing and pointing as they glanced back at Matt. They walked into the garage, and its door growled open. The truck's engine started, then faded as it backed out and drove away.

Chapter Eight

MATT TRIED TO SILENCE the pounding of his heart and the sparking of his nerves, but it was difficult. The staircase seemed longer and steeper than he ever knew, the steps like teeth. He felt like he was about to hurtle down the stairs if he simply took a breath. He focused on his breathing, and after what seemed years, he calmed down.

The first thing he had to do was to move away from the staircase. He put his feet next to one leg of the base, cautiously swiveling toward the railing. Pulling up his knees, he pushed off a banister with his feet. The chair rolled back from the steps. He released a breath of relief.

Matt frantically fought against the tape but stopped when he realized it didn't accomplish a thing. He tried again, slower this time and with all his strength. He could feel his muscles straining as he panted with the effort. Beads of sweat broke out on his forehead. No sign he was making any progress, so he gave up on plan A. He had to try something else.

Inch by inch, he scooted his chair down the hall and back into his room, ending up with his right arm next to his desk. The goon left the top drawer open. Matt had enough freedom in his hand to reach in and fumble for a pair of scissors. He maneuvered the blades toward the bindings on his right wrist. They were too long and reached up his forearm. They couldn't bite on the tape and start cutting. He growled in frustration and dropped the scissors. Time for plan C. He looked around, and his eyes fell on the dish containing his phone.

Matt pushed himself over to the nightstand. He reached for the casserole dish. His fingers only brushed the air. He battled against his bonds, gritting his teeth in the effort. The tape binding his wrist didn't permit enough movement, the plastic digging into his skin. The dish remained just out of reach, taunting him with its proximity.

He rolled the chair a little away and then leaned back. Lifting his feet off the floor, he planted them on the nightstand. In awkward, jerky spurts and hops, he moved his heels toward the dish. He nudged it nearer to the side.

The dish continued to slide across the wood top as he pushed harder. Almost there. The dish teetered at the edge of the nightstand. Matt put his feet back on the floor.

He positioned the chair next to the dish and stretched out his fingers, straining against the tape on his wrist. The casserole balanced precariously; the slightest incorrect movement could send it crashing into his lap or the ground, rendering it completely out of reach.

Matt tried again. He reached for one of the dish's tab handles, letting out a laugh of relief when he closed his fingers around it. Then slowly, carefully, he began to tug it off the nightstand. *Easy does it, easy does it ...* He performed the task with the same care as though defusing a bomb.

The dish suddenly slipped. Matt made a desperate grab for his phone, barely catching hold of the very bottom of it before the dish landed in his lap, then continued its journey to the floor, smashing his toes and spewing rice everywhere. He grimaced and swore.

Gingerly working his grasp higher on his prize, he pressed the power button. To his relief, it booted. He laid his phone back on the nightstand, his bound wrist allowing his index finger just enough movement to access the screen.

Unlocking the phone, he sent a text to Hunter: "c2 mah house asap."

A response came through a few minutes later: "at wedding wl come in aboot three hrs."

Matt leaned his head against the back of the chair. Time to hurry up and wait.

Hunter's voice drifted up from the kitchen door downstairs. "Matt? Where are you?"

Matt gave a muffled yell and stomped his feet on the floor. He heard Hunter climbing the stairs.

"I see the garage is open. Did Trent get his truck back? How did ..." his voice trailed off as he entered Matt's bedroom and took in the scene. He recovered rapidly and planted his fists on his hips. "I can't leave you alone for a second, can I?"

Matt responded with a muffled swear word, followed by kicking the scissors toward his friend. Picking them up, Hunter cut and peeled the adhesive from one side of Matt's mouth.

"Does this happen to the Hardy Boys?" Matt asked.

"Frequently, although not to this extent." Hunter gazed at all the tape a little tentatively, as though unsure where to start. "Getting all this stuff off will probably hurt. It'll be like yanking off a bandage."

"No worries, just get me loose," Matt grumbled.

Face set in grim determination, Hunter worked, snipping and pulling the tape. Matt grimaced and winced, feeling as though his flesh was being stripped off as the tape loosened.

"There. Done." Hunter stepped back and put the scissors on the desk.

"Thanks." Matt stood and stretched. He couldn't help but notice the absurdity of the differences in their dress: Hunter in one of his suits, sporting a blinding yellow tie, and Matt in his boxer shorts. "Like, how was the wedding?"

"Boring. Your text came through while the bride and groom were reading sloppy, badly written love poems to each other." Hunter held up the ball of tape in an unspoken question.

"I had some visitors." Matt pulled on his pants and headed to the bathroom. Hunter followed, dunking the adhesive into the trash can.

"Two points! I figured that, unless you are remarkably agile." Hunter crossed his arms and leaned against the doorjamb.

"Then I bet you can figure out who they were, Sherlock." Matt took a washcloth and washed the dried blood from the cut under his eye.

"Easy. The Black Sedan Boys," Hunter replied. "But what did they want?"

"More stuff about the USB drive," Matt answered. "The great graduate assistant didn't like the 'found it out yonder in the north forty' answer."

"How did they find you? We never told our names," Hunter said.

"I put mine down on the interest list in the Admissions Office," Matt said. "I'm sure Sokolov easily could get a copy."

"There must have been others on that page," Hunter said.

"Yeah, but they could ditch some immediately. Females, for instance, or people from out of state," Matt stated. "The Black Sedan Boys must have had orders to check out the leftovers on the list. They struck gold when they spotted the truck."

"So those two are tied up with the Sleep Clinic and Richter. Pardon the pun," Hunter mused, "they work for him."

Matt shook his head. "I think Sokolov is their employer. Richter is in Germany on sabbatical, remember? Those things are like one semester long. So if Richter is part of this, he's left calling the shots to Sokolov."

"There are phones," Hunter pointed out. "Germany is not on another planet."

"True." Matt remembered what he saw last night. "I still believe Sokolov is running the show."

"Based on what?"

Matt hesitated, not wanting to tell Hunter what happened at the Clinic. "Because of yesterday. The way Sokolov acted."

Hunter didn't pick up on the hesitation. "So the Black Sedan Boys took the truck also?"

"Ding! You can level up." Matt returned the washcloth to the rack.

"Why did they want it? It doesn't seem they need another set of wheels."

Matt's thoughts darted to the jammer he hid in the garage and wondered how much to let Hunter know. He wanted to tell him everything but didn't have an idea where that would end up. He punted. "Don't ask me. Maybe they mow lawns as a side gig."

He picked up the disbelief in Hunter's mind as he brushed past him on the way to his room. He understood his friend was waiting for him to elaborate, but Matt couldn't string together what else to say.

Matt sat on his bed and put on his socks and shoes. He pulled a clean tee-shirt out of a dresser drawer and slipped it on. Hunter stood by the nightstand, hands stuffed into his pockets.

"Bro, honest people make terrible liars," Hunter observed. "Okay, the Black Sedan Boys paid you a house call, but there's more in the script. You're not telling me something."

"I told you everything," Matt snapped as he snatched his dirty tee-shirt off the floor and turned away from the door. Hunter's eyes were burning into his back. He looked down at the garment in his hands. He had twisted it into a wad.

"Dude, I found you in your shorts, duct-taped to a chair! You're hiding something from me!" Hunter shouted. He calmed down, and Matt faced him. "Look, you're my buddy. You're mixed in some trouble. I want to help, but you need to come clean with me. Are you messed up in some type of drug thing?"

"Drugs?" Matt laughed out loud, but it was a bitter laugh. "Those shrinks shoved so many meds on me, I can't take an aspirin." He sat heavily on the bed, sinking down into the mattress. He drew a deep breath. "All right, all right, here it is, straight up."

He told Hunter about his previous night's trip to the Sleep Clinic and what he had witnessed there. Hunter stood with his mouth open when Matt finished. It took him a second to find his voice.

"Dude ... dude, you need to call the cops!" Urgency and fear laced Hunter's voice.

"No," Matt returned in a resolute and final tone.

"You're kidding!" Hunter's hands flew up in the air in frustration. "Like, there's auto theft—"

"I stole the truck first, if you want to get technical about it."

"All right, fine, fine." Hunter's voice was incredulous, and he shook his head as he spoke. He counted off on his fingers. "Then how about little things like kidnapping, home invasion, torture? Felonies all, most likely."

Matt stood. He was emphatic. "I said no cops."

"You're crazy!" Hunter cried.

"I could hook you up with a bunch of people who agree with you," Matt fired back. There was an awkward silence.

"I'm sorry. I didn't mean it that way."

Matt sighed. "I know."

"You told the Black Sedan Boys the USB drive was in the truck, right?" Hunter asked. Matt nodded. "Then why swipe the pickup? I still don't get it."

Matt waited for a moment, knowing that his friend would connect the dots. He did.

Hunter took a few steps forward. "They would only take the truck because they're looking for something else they think is hidden in it, something other than the drive."

"Bingo."

Hunter thought for a few more moments, then grinned. "Well, they'll find what they want, so we won't see them—"

"Except they won't." Matt sprawled in the chair.

"They won't? Why not?"

"Because I had the object of their desire in my pocket the whole time we searched the truck," Matt admitted. "The thing is still here in the house."

"Well, what is it?" Hunter asked in exasperation. "A thermonuclear device that will end civilization? Something that predicts winning lottery numbers? Or do I have to play twenty questions instead?"

Matt could talk his way around Hunter's inquiries; he'd done that for years in therapy. Hunter was his friend, and he needed one now. Matt didn't want to lie to him, but he couldn't afford to tell the complete truth, either. He was stuck in the middle, not knowing what to do.

"It is a highly specialized device, but not of mass destruction." Matt selected his words carefully as he stood. The cat was partially out of the bag, wriggling and howling to be released all the way. Matt hoped some plausible, halfway correct explanation that would stuff it back inside would occur to him while they walked downstairs. "Come on. I'll show you."

Matt led Hunter to the garage, hitting the button to close the rolling door. When it shut, he grabbed the coffee can and dumped the contents on the workbench. He held up the black box. "This is what I think the Black Sedan Boys and Sokolov are after."

Hunter leaned forward and peered at it. "What is it?"

"A jammer." Matt turned the object over in his hands.

"Well, what does it jam? Wi-Fi? Cell signals? Radio? What?" Hunter shrugged.

Matt's heart was pounding as he realized there was no turning back now. Everything would have to come out. He had no clue how Hunter would react, and the thought made him queasy. "This thing is a neural-pulsomic-jammer."

"Lovely name. Sounds like a specialty coffee." Hunter pushed his glasses back up his nose. "But what does that gizmo block?"

Matt showed the power switch. "When it's on, this hides brain waves."

"Brain waves?" Hunter shook his head in confusion.

"Yes, brain waves." *Here goes,* Matt thought. He took a deep breath. "This jammer prevents people from reading minds."

"Reading minds!" Hunter tried to suppress a smile. "This is what Trent said?"

Matt nodded uncomfortably.

"Like, did he use this gadget to stop people from reading his mind or him from reading other people's minds?" Hunter was struggling to keep a straight face.

"Both." Matt was realizing how silly this whole thing must sound. Maybe he was wrong to tell Hunter this much.

"Was he wearing his tin foil hat when he told you?" One corner of Hunter's mouth turned up in a smile.

"Don't be—"

"Oh come, Matt, please." Hunter giggled. "You meet a complete stranger on the trail and he tells you he can read minds?"

"Yes." It was sounding dumber and dumber the more it came out.

"And you bought it?" Hunter snorted. "Hey, I know where you can get your hands on some crypto. Cheap too."

"Why else would the Black Sedan Boys be after him?"

"They're probably attendants from a nuthouse," Hunter said. "The nice young men in clean white coats."

"That's not so! Trent reads minds!" Matt yelled.

"What trash!" Hunter walked away a few steps, then came back. "How can you swallow something as wild as that? Like, how ludicrous!"

"It's not! He's telepathic! No cap!" Matt shot back.

"How do you know?" Hunter sounded like a prosecuting attorney questioning a hostile witness, as he jabbed his index finger at Matt. "Because he told you? You believe everything you're told? Is that why? How do you know? Well? How do you? Huh? Tell me!"

"Because I can read minds too!" Matt angrily blurted out.

Chapter Nine

THERE. HE DID IT. The secret was out.

Matt felt oddly comfortable, even relieved, that he said it. He knew that this could change everything, possibly pitching him back into a downward spiral of psychiatrist couches and medications. If Hunter remained a friend, he may not look at him the same way again. He was unsure if he was ready for that.

He watched the expected reactions parade across Hunter's face: a smile, as though what he said was a joke, followed by confusion, concern, and the last one, the one Matt absolutely detested: pity. The same pity held for a small animal caught in a trap, futilely struggling against the implacable iron grip. The pity of someone who knew they could do nothing to help, who was just waiting for the animal to give up and die already. It was a pity that made Matt angry.

"Don't look at me like that! Please! I can't stand it! I don't want your sanctimonious understanding or the clucking of your tongue as you oh so delicately suggest I 'see someone,' while slowly backing away like I have Ebola. Stuff your pity. I don't need it." Matt slapped the garage door button. Over the grumbling of the motor, he yelled, "Now get out! Out! Go away! Leave me alone! And take your pity with you."

Matt spun away from Hunter and rubbed his eyes. They stung. The door suddenly reversed direction. He looked over his shoulder. Hunter stood by the switch.

"You're not getting rid of me that easily," Hunter said.

Matt faced his friend and smiled.

Hunter spread his hands. "I'm an actor. Every time I step onstage, I have to make the unbelievable believable to an audience ... that I'm older than I am, or the greatest lover in all of history. So, convince me. What am I thinking?"

"Too easy," Matt replied. "It's written all over your face in letters ten feet tall. Think of something totally weird."

"What?"

"Picture in your mind something ridiculous, like, absurd. Go on, use your imagination. You got one."

Hunter nodded.

Matt moved closer. For a second, it seemed Hunter was going to retreat, but he stayed put.

"A twelve-foot-tall purple rabbit eating a tutti-fruity ice cream cone while looking at the Mona Lisa," Matt reported.

The expression on Hunter's face showed he was correct.

"Now recall a thing that happened in your past, something you never told me." Matt closed his eyes and chuckled. He opened them again. "You're five years old. You and your mother waited in line to see Santa Claus for over an hour. When it was finally your turn, you got scared and started crying. Your mother got pissed. And no, I won't tell anybody."

Hunter's eyes were wide, his lips parted slightly in shock. His eyebrows were raised, giving him the look of a child witnessing his first magic trick.

Matt smiled. "Ah, at last, you're impressed."

Hunter sputtered something. A salad of words came out. Then he fell silent. He reminded Matt of a video he once saw of old-fashioned computers, lights blinking wildly as it solved a problem. His friend was like one that was on the verge of overload, attempting to process too much information at once and shutting down. To give Hunter some privacy, Matt moved away and put the jammer on the workbench. He leaned against the plywood top and crossed his arms, waiting.

"Okay ... okay ..." Hunter focused on the floor and held his hands out in front of him, as though trying to remain steady on the deck of a pitching ship. He was speaking out loud but was really talking to himself. "I have a friend who reads minds. Okay ... all right ... I can deal with this ... right ... yes." He took a deep breath and met Matt's gaze. "So in the years we've known each other, you read my mind? Heard my thoughts?"

"Not always," Matt said. "I have to be within a few feet of a person."

"I mean ... wow." Hunter ran a hand through his hair, making it frizz out in an even more gravity-defying way, still staring at Matt in disbelief. "I did not know. I just figured you were great at reading people."

"I don't talk about it. Like, the usual response is a freak out if I do," Matt continued sarcastically, "that's how I ended up under the care of trained professionals."

"You must have told somebody about this, then proved you could. As you did with me," Hunter argued.

Matt's lips twisted into a wry smile. "Once, with one of my first therapists. We had a good 'therapeutic rapport', I think it's called. So I just said I could read minds, and then I told him exactly what he was thinking. Word for word." His smile faded. "He flipped. The guy became unglued, completely terrified. He gaped at me like I was a demon who'd popped right out of the Old Testament. I quickly lied that it was only a magic trick I learned. I pretended to blow the next try at mind reading to calm him down. Every session after that, he made some lame joke about it, but he was still uneasy around me. You're the only other person who knows, except Trent."

"But, Matt, what a gift—" Hunter began.

"Gift!" Matt spat out. "I have a curse, dude, not a gift! It's not like the movies." He placed two fingers of both hands on his temples and spoke in a spooky voice. "'I'm going to read your mind now.'" He dropped his hands and moved away from the workbench. "I can't control it. If I'm near enough to somebody—bam!—what's in their brains ram into mine. Ready or not, here they come."

"That is why you are so tense at an assembly? You seem like a grenade about to explode. Is it everybody packed around you?" Hunter asked.

Matt nodded. "Their thoughts swamp my head at once. I also sit in the back corner of classes. I only have to deal with the kid at the desk directly in front."

"Wow. Here I thought you had a case of social anxiety," Hunter said.

"That's perhaps the one label that hasn't been pasted on my forehead," Matt said dryly. He pleaded with Hunter, "Dude, please don't tell anybody. Please. I beg you. It would cause—"

"No worries," Hunter said. "You keep the Santa story low-key, and I won't spill the tea about your, um ... special skill. Deal?" He stuck out his hand.

Matt shook it and grinned. "Deal."

"Trent and I are the only ones that know about you." A worried expression crossed Hunter's face. "Along with Sokolov and Richter?"

"I'm sure Sokolov is on to Trent. Why else kidnap him?" Matt paced as he talked. "But I'm not sure that he's made up his mind about me. I don't think so. He may be sus about me, but he doesn't want to risk grabbing me. Like, I'm a local, and if I suddenly disappear, someone might notice it. Certainly by my parents when they get back. Trent isn't from anywhere around here, so his family would need to file a missing person's report. That could take a month or longer." He considered things for a moment. "The one guy I'm not clear about is Richter. Like, how he fits into all this."

"The Black Sedan Boys? What about those tools? Are they on to the truth?"

Matt gave a derisive laugh. "Those two can't generate enough voltage to light up an LED bulb between them. Hired hands only."

"They search the truck and come up empty-handed and—" Hunter ventured.

"They'll try to force Trent to tell them where the jammer is," Matt finished and shivered. "It won't be pretty. I've seen their methods in action."

"Except Trent doesn't know the device's location," noted Hunter.

Matt shook his head. "He saw it last in his backpack. Eventually, they will have to believe he's telling the truth.

Then there is only one option open: they make a return visit here." He held up a hand. "Before you again say call the police, which you were about to, it won't help. The cops won't put around-the-clock surveillance on this house for two guys I can't describe who might show up at some unknown time in the future."

"You can always go stand next to Sokolov. Maybe he'll throw a random thought where Trent is," Hunter tossed off.

Matt snapped his fingers. "Facts! But I'll do that with the Black Sedan Boys, not Sokolov. If I get them to bring Trent to mind ..."

"How are you going to do that?"

"Simple. Just ask them. They won't tell me in words, of course, but they'll think about the answer. Like, try not to think about an elephant when I say don't think about an elephant," Matt explained.

"How do we reach them? Wait for the next break?" Hunter asked. "Text them?"

Matt held up the jammer. "Here's how. They can track the location of this thing when powered on. They found Trent that way. We'll turn it on and just let them come to us. But where and when we choose."

The Chamber of Commerce website insisted that the Midtown section was 'in transition'. Sturdy brick buildings constructed in the early twentieth century lined the two-lane street. The occasional tree, almost seeming a mistake, interspersed the storefronts. Trendy coffee places, with names like 'Java Alley' and 'Brew Cafe', pointedly ignored the neighboring tattoo parlors, dive bars, and tired motels. The smell of sizzling burgers wafted from the open doors of the cheap diners, mingled with exotic smells from tiny bistros which served small, artfully arranged portions on over-sized plates. The sound of laughter, loud talking, music, and glasses clinking stumbled out of the bars.

The area was popular with the chic folk, and the trendy crowded the street, moving in all directions. While not as packed as when the university was in session, many groups streamed in and out of the various businesses. Cars honked and brakes squealed. Voices yelled. The air was thick with exhaust and the odor of frying food.

Matt pulled into a parking place in the early evening. "The saying goes 'safety in numbers'. Our friends may not try any rough stuff in front of so many witnesses."

Hunter nodded in response. He took something out of his pocket. It was a small black box the size of a packet of cards.

Matt grinned. "Dude, that is an exact copy of the jammer. I can't believe you built that in one day."

"It wasn't tough to make," Hunter replied. "Like, the thing is only a box painted black with a switch on it. You can see it's a prop from close up, but not from a distance. It'll fool them if we need a distraction."

Matt patted his pocket, which held the actual device. "Remember the plan. When we start walking, I'll turn on the jammer, and we wait for them to approach. I'll ask where they're holding Trent. As soon as I get the answer, I'll let you know. Pull out the fake jammer and toss it as far away as possible. The Black Sedan Boys will go after it like

dogs fetching a stick. We take off in the opposite direction. Ready?"

Hunter smiled and put on a deerstalker hat. He nodded. "The game's afoot, Watson."

The two climbed out of the car. Matt flipped the
switch on the jammer and returned the device to his
pocket, then he and Hunter walked down the block. The
night was warm. Music spilled out of the open doors of
the shops and restaurants as they passed. Several groups
of people, some chatting among themselves and some
paying particular attention to their phones and nothing
else, strolled by. A large group of men wearing fashion-
ably retro tie-dyed t-shirts and jeans approached from
the other direction, laughing loudly and working hard
to make sure everybody knew they were having a good
time.

"I've never seen you more relaxed in a crowd," Hunter
observed.

Matt smiled and nodded. "The miracle of modern
electronics."

The two strolled both sides of the five blocks making
up the district, keeping an eye out for the black sedan.
Nothing showed. They stopped in a cafe for an over-
priced cup of mediocre coffee, sipping the hot drink
among the distressed brick walls, hanging plants, and
the jazz version of elevator music.

"That thing does track, doesn't it? Like, it actually
works?" Hunter asked.

"Trent said so." Matt took a swallow, his gaze trained
out the window.

"Are you sure it's turned on?"

Matt rolled his eyes. "Come on, dude. It only has one switch."

Draining their cups, they went back on the sidewalk and made another circle, finally stepping inside a tiny art gallery. The young woman at the desk didn't bother to glance up from her phone. Matt was examining an abstract painting, wondering if the artist was seven or eight years old, when Hunter nudged him. "Outside."

Matt turned and watched a black sedan cruise by. "That's them," he said, his voice low. "It's showtime."

The friends returned to the street. The sedan was pulling into a parking spot a couple of blocks up. Matt started moving, Hunter beside him, casually walking toward the black car. As they passed, Hunter took the fake jammer out of his pocket, tossed it in the air, and caught it, making sure his action was obvious to the two men sitting in the sedan. It was. Car doors opened and closed behind Matt and Hunter.

"Here they come. Make an about-face... now!" Matt and Hunter abruptly changed direction and returned the way they came.

"Well?" Hunter asked. "Is that them?"

Matt nodded. "They wore ski masks last I saw them, but their build is the same."

"They're huge!" Hunter gasped.

The two men had beardless chins and close-cropped hair. They were young, probably no older than the students at the university. They were, or could have been, football players there. Their clothes, made of thick, sturdy fabric, seemed like they would rip at the seams from all the muscle packed under them. They walked with the easy swagger of those who were sure of their high status and knew they deserved it. The pairs met and stopped.

"Hey," Matt greeted. "I didn't expect to see you guys. You look different without your masks. I can't decide if it's an improvement or not. Like, you down here to buy more duct tape? Say, how many likes did your video rack up?"

"You little ..." the young man on the left growled and stepped forward.

"Ah, ah, ah." Matt wagged a reproaching finger, then pointed. "There's a black and white about a block in back of you."

Hunter leaned in and added in a helpful whisper, "Don't check behind you, either. It might seem strange."

The two goons remained glumly silent. "Jesse," the first one commanded the other in a quiet voice.

Jesse went next to Hunter as though to talk to him, casting a sidelong glance down the street. He gave a curt nod to the other man.

"Is that settled? Splendid. I have a simple question for you." Matt moved into range of the man in front of him. "Where have you got my friend, Trent?"

Matt could read the answer forming in the other's mind when the second man called out. "Cole, the cop car's turned the corner!"

Jesse grabbed Hunter's hand, the one hanging on to the fake jammer. Hunter wrenched free and backed out of reach.

"Say, you, yeah, you, big bruiser," Hunter taunted. He held up the black box and wiggled it back and forth. "Does baby want the pretty toy, huh? Does he? Come and get it!"

Hunter took off down the street. His smaller size helped him dart and weave through the crowd, Jesse following like a lumbering tank.

The man in front of Matt was about to join the pursuit. Matt couldn't let the two go after Hunter and possibly hurt him. He had to peel this one off. Matt pulled out the real jammer and held it up so it was clearly visible to Cole. He spoke in an overly polite way. "Could this be what you're looking for?"

Cole made a lunge. Matt dodged the man, turned, jammed the device into his pocket, and ran. Cole came after him, his feet pounding the ground with the steady, rhythmic beat of a drum, like hands clapping in unison. The crowd whistled, yelled, and jeered as they barreled through them. Matt couldn't outrun somebody as athletic as Cole for long. It was only a matter of time before Cole caught him; he had to do something different to throw off his pursuer. He ducked into a dark, narrow alley between two buildings. Graffiti covered the walls and trash cans and dumpsters stood by the back doors.

Cole was gaining. He reached out and grabbed Matt's shoulder, spinning him around until he had backed him up against the filthy brick wall next to some door. Matt twisted free of Cole's grasp and stumbled sideways into a doorway. The man followed, throwing a heavy fist that glanced off Matt's arm. Matt ducked, whirled around, clutched both hands in a hammer, and brought them straight up into Cole's chin with all his strength. The man's head snapped back, and he staggered halfway across the alleyway with an almost comical 'oof'. Matt kicked himself away from the wall and darted behind Cole as the big man regained his balance and turned towards him once more. Matt swept Cole's legs out from under him with one swift kick to the knees, dropping him to the pavement. In another moment, he had an empty trashcan in hand and jammed it over his pursuer's head, catching it on his broad shoulders. Locking his arms together on top of the can, Matt jumped up and down twice, wedging it tight. A flurry of muffled swearing hollowly echoed out.

Matt's heart pounded in his chest as he raced back toward the street. He was wheezing and huffing, and his legs burned from sprinting so hard. The black sedan turned into the alley. Its lights hit Matt, freezing him as a living example of a deer in the headlights. The car crept past a dumpster, squeezing between it and the brick wall opposite. The sedan stopped, blocking Matt's path. Behind him, the trash can crashed onto the asphalt.

Matt glanced over his shoulder. Cole was on his feet. He held his arms slightly away from his body, his fingers cramped like claws. He gave out a wordless, angry growl, more animal than human.

Chapter Ten

"GRAB HIM, JESSE!" COLE called out.

Jesse pushed the car door open and climbed out. Matt ran toward the sedan, pumping his legs harder and harder. He tossed the jammer in the driver's direction. "Heads up, Jesse!"

Matt grunted as he dove on the car's hood, piling into the windshield. Scrambling, he continued over the roof and slid off the trunk. He pulled some garbage cans onto the pavement behind the sedan. His heart was pounding in his chest, and he gasped as breath stole back into his lungs. He slowed to walk as he reached the sidewalk and merged with the crowds, smoothing out his rumpled clothes.

"How was it, man?" a guy called out.

Matt smiled and flashed the thumbs up. The other man chortled knowingly.

Matt pulled out his phone and texted Hunter: "r u all rite."

He was relieved by an answer returned almost immediately: "w8ing by j00r car."

Grinning as he pocketed his cell, Matt jogged up the sidewalk. Hunter leaned against his car's fender.

"What happened?" Hunter asked.

Matt climbed into the driver's seat. He turned towards his friend as he got into the passenger side of the car. "Let's peace out," he said. "I can't drive, listen, and make sure we're not followed at the same time."

He pulled into traffic, made a few quick turns, and checked his rearview mirror. He kept looking until he was positive he was not pursued. He couldn't believe what had happened. The adrenaline and excitement from the encounter with the Black Sedan Boys had worn off, leaving him with an empty feeling of defeat. Nothing had gone right. His mind replayed the evening, trying to figure out where he had gone wrong.

"Let's get something to eat," Hunter suggested.

"Eat? Seriously?"

"Yeah. You always go out to eat after a performance," Hunter said. "It's a great theatrical tradition."

"What we just did was a performance?" Matt shot back.

"Wasn't it?"

"Go and eat, even if what we performed was a thumping failure?" Matt's voice was bitter.

"Maybe not," Hunter hinted.

After throwing a questioning glance at Hunter, Matt swung into a lot of a fast-food joint. He parked next to a huge RV, which blocked the view of his car from the street. He killed the engine and turned to Hunter. "All right. Let's go inside and get something to eat, then give ourselves a review."

They found a booth in the back of the dining room after picking up their orders. The table was sticky, and the surrounding air carried the faint aroma of bleach.

Matt told Hunter what had happened to him.

"So they got the jammer?" Hunter asked as he popped a french fry into his mouth. His eyes narrowed in concentration, and his brow furrowed.

"I was boxed in. They were going to get that jammer, period. I picked the way with the least chance of bodily injury." Matt morosely stirred his soda with the straw and sighed. "It was a good way to find out about Trent. It just didn't work. I got nothing at the Sleep Clinic yesterday and zip tonight. Strike two."

"You didn't pick up anything? I mean, you couldn't read anything?" Hunter took a bite of his bacon cheeseburger. He grabbed a napkin to wipe some grease off his chin.

Matt shook his head. "The thought was just forming in what passes for Cole's brain. I saw Trent in a room, dark gray, nothing more definite. When Jesse called out about the cop car, Cole turned his attention to that, then the image disappeared."

"Bummerific."

"No cap. We're no closer to finding Trent than when we began," Matt sat back in his seat, crossing his arms. "I heard an old expression once about a hospital. The operation was a success but the patient died."

"Perhaps we can resuscitate that patient," Hunter offered.

Matt raised his eyebrows in a question.

"Black Sedan Boy number two, I guess his proper name is Jesse, dragged me into another alley and slammed me against the wall. We struggled over the fake jammer until I threw it farther down the pavement. I grabbed his shirt pocket when he turned to go after it, and it tore. Something interesting fell out." Hunter took a bite of his cheeseburger, eyes bright with mischief.

Matt sat up, interested. The gloom of failure started lifting. "Well, what, what was it, you little dweeb? Are you going to tell me? Spill."

Hunter leaned forward, pulled a business card out of his hip pocket, and slid it across the table, then sucked on his milkshake, waiting for Matt's reaction.

The card pictured an attractive bikini-clad girl holding up two frothy tankards of beer. "The 'Babe-O-Licious Gentleman's Club'?" Matt read the heading out loud and snorted. "There's an oxymoron."

"Bonus points for the college prep word, but it tells something about the Black Sedan Boys." Hunter sat back in his seat.

"How do you know that? Enlighten me." Matt picked up his soda.

"That card is one of those 'buy-ten-get-one-free' punch things. For a free beer, I suppose," Hunter explained.

"Maybe it's for the waitress," Matt interjected.

"Shut up, you neanderthal ninny." Hunter twirled a finger. "Now, check out the back side. Of the card, not the waitress."

Matt did as he was told. "There's a date stamped on the back."

Hunter leaned forward and tapped the card. "Most likely when the card was first issued. What is that date?"

"About a week and a half ago," Matt did some quick math and added, "Ten days."

"Correct." Hunter waved a french fry at the card. "Now, how many holes are punched? You can count that high, can't you?"

"I'll try, but I may need some help past two." Matt flipped the card over. "Seven."

"Now, read the fine print above the numbers," Hunter said, munching on a fry. He picked up a small packet and complained, "Needs salt."

Matt held the card up to his eyes and squinted at the tiny type. "It says 'limit one punch per visit.'"

"Now we put all this together to make some deductions," Hunter dumped the entire contents of the salt package on his fries. "First, The Black Sedan Boys are, shall we say, members in good standing at the Babe-O-Licious Gentleman's Club. Second, they are frequent customers of said club. How do we know this, you may ask?" Hunter took a dramatic pause.

"Okay, okay, I'm asking already," Matt prompted.

"Elementary, my dear Watson, elementary." Hunter sat back in his seat with his arms spread wide. He noted Matt's expression and tapped the deerstalker, adding, "I played Sherlock Holmes in a youth theater production a couple of summers back."

"Well, I'm glad something rubbed off."

Hunter went on, "The card is a mere ten days old, but already punched seven times. Since the user can get only one punch at a time ..." He gestured for Matt to pick up the thread.

"... the Black Sedan Boys are probably going to pay a return visit to the club. Soon," Matt finished.

"Like, I'm sure they want that free beer." Hunter returned the card to his pocket and performed a theatrical sigh. "Alas, although poor old Jesse will have to start all over."

Matt became excited as he sat up. "Okay, okay, here's the plan. They have the jammer, so in their minds, they're done with us, but we're not with them. We'll go to that club—"

Hunter shook his head. "We can't get in there. It's an over-21 joint."

"Fine, we'll wait for them outside then, starting tomorrow night, and go the next night and the next one if we have to, pick them up and follow them, for a change. They may take us straight to Trent."

Matt yawned and stretched as far as the interior of his mother's car would permit. He figured the Black Sedan Boys would know his ride by now, so he borrowed his mom's beige-mobile. It was so bland it would be forgotten as soon as a person looked away. He flicked the pine tree-shaped air freshener hanging from the rear-view mirror with his finger.

Picking his phone off the passenger seat, he checked the time: 12:07 am. With a groan, he put his phone down and leaned his head against the backrest, letting out his breath. Detective work was more exciting in the movies. He stared at the Babe-O-Licious Club on the far side of the poorly maintained, pot-holed patch of asphalt.

The windowless building squatted at the edge of an area made up of warehouses and small manufacturing firms. It must have been an Italian restaurant once, judging from the now-faded murals of Tuscany vineyards that adorned its walls. The only image that appeared to be fresh was one of a beautiful blonde, for some inexplicable reason riding a wine keg as though it were a bucking bronco. Stuccoed arches topped with plastic roofing tiles sat about a foot away from the box-like main structure. The arches held light bulbs that would blink on, then slowly change colors from red to white to blue to green. Cement urns, some empty and a few containing struggling cypress trees lined the front of the place. In case the club's name alone didn't describe the business inside, bright orange paint promised GIRLS! GIRLS! GIRLS! along the bottom of the sign.

The crowded, badly lit parking lot seemed to hold every type of vehicle, from big rigs to cars that made Matt's look like a Rolls-Royce, plus everything in between, including a particular black German sports sedan. Even though Matt parked in the farthest corner of the pavement, he still felt, more than heard, the thump... thump... thump of the bass from the club's sound system.

The walkie-talkie laying on the passenger seat next to Matt's phone crackled, "Hardy One to Hardy Two ... Hardy One to Hardy Two ... come in, please."

Grabbing the two-way radio, Matt pressed the Talk button. "Yeah, Hunter?"

There was only static for a second, followed by an exasperated, "Matt ..."

Matt rolled his eyes. He first thought the idea of radios was silly, but finally agreed that they would be a faster way to communicate than using their phones. He pushed the button again. "Hardy Two to Hardy One. I copy. Over."

"Is the quail still in the nest?" Hunter over-articulated each word. "Repeat: is the quail still in the nest? Over."

"The quail are still in the nest, but the nest closes in two hours," Matt reported. He quickly tacked on, "over."

"So does my curfew. Roger, I copy. Over and out."

Matt chuckled as he put down the walkie-talkie. The smile faded as he worried about Trent. He shifted in his seat in a futile attempt to get more comfortable and yawned.

The club's exit swung open, pulsating music and laughing voices assaulting the night. A boisterous group of men stepped outside. The door closed behind them, cloaking them in shadows. Matt sat up. He thought he spotted the Black Sedan Boys among them, but he couldn't be positive in the darkness.

With one final, backslapping guffaw, the group broke up, the members strolling in all directions. Two of them went toward the black sedan. Matt strained his eyes as he looked, making sure it was Cole and Jesse. They tossed a glance at Matt's car. He threw himself down across the passenger seat. He remembered a joke Hunter had played on him and repeated the action so it was just visible over the dash: he wrapped his arms around himself, caressing his hair and back with his hands. Hissing laughs and calls of 'Go get 'er!' came from the Black Sedan Boys as they walked by.

Matt was on top of the radio, the handset pressing into his stomach. He finished his performance and fished it out. "Hunter ... Hunter ... they're... uh, Hardy Two to Hardy One, Hardy Two to Hardy One, come in, please."

Hunter's voice came through the static, tinny, and distant. "Hardy One to Hardy Two. I copy. Over."

"Sshhh!" Matt clutched the radio with both hands and moved it tight against his lips, thinking that would stop the Black Sedan Boys from hearing him, although they were a good twenty feet away. "The quail have—"

"Hardy Two, back off the mic! You're distorting!"

"Sorry." Matt pulled the walkie-talkie away from his mouth. He spoke softly, but excitedly, "I repeat, the chickens have flown the nest. No, the quail have left the coop—"

"What?"

"I mean, the quail has left the nest." He risked a peek over the dashboard. "They just got into their car. Stand by."

The black sedan's engine throbbed to life. The car's brake lights flared, and it backed out of its parking spot.

Matt ducked behind the dash again as the sedan drove past him. "Hardy Two to Hardy One. They're on the move. Repeat: the quail are taking flight." He sat up. "And so are we."

Chapter Eleven

COLE AND JESSE'S CAR braked briefly at the parking lot exit, the right turn indicator blinking.

Matt pushed the radio's Talk button. "Hardy One, they're turning right on Fourth. Over."

"Hardy Two, I'm parked on Jackson. That will take them right past me," Hunter said. "I'll pick them up. Over." The sound of Hunter's SUV starting came over the radio.

"Hardy One, they've made the turn."

There was a pause, then Hunter spoke, "They just drove by. I'm going to follow them."

"Stay a good distance behind them. Don't crowd them," Matt cautioned. "There's not much traffic this late. I'll take Third up to Madison to get ahead of them, then I'll pull behind you. You turn off and head for Wilson. We'll switch there again."

"Roger. Hardy One out," Hunter clicked off.

Matt's hands gripped the wheel as he started his engine, pressed his foot down on the gas pedal, and zoomed to Third Street. His headlights illuminated the front of the dark buildings crowding the pavement, silent spectators at a stock car race. He didn't slow down as he bumped over a set of railroad tracks, the car trembling and threatening to shake apart. Completely ignoring a stop sign, he turned at Third and Madison, pulled to the side, and shut off his lights.

"Come on, come on, where are you?" Matt mumbled to himself. His fingers drummed on the wheel as he leaned forward to peer into the night.

The sedan sped by, followed by the SUV. Matt switched on his headlights, and swung on Fourth, dropping into position behind Hunter. Matt felt around for the walkie-talkie and grasped it.

"Hardy Two to Hardy One," Matt said into the radio. "Check your mirror. I'm behind you."

"Hardy One to Hardy Two," responded Hunter, "I see you. I'll make a right at the next block, go up to Wilson and wait for further instructions."

"I copy, Hardy One. Out." Matt returned the unit to his passenger seat.

Hunter's SUV signaled, then turned off the street. Matt sped up slightly to keep his prey in sight. The street now widened to four lanes, and more traffic appeared, allowing Matt to maintain a car between him and the one he was trailing. After a few miles, the sedan turned into the lot of an all-night convenience store. Matt continued to the next block and parked, letting the engine idle. He grabbed the radio.

"Hardy Two to Hardy One." Part of Matt wanted to drop the call signals, but it now felt it was the correct thing to do.

"Hardy One. I copy."

"They just entered the Grab-It Store on Fourth. I guess they craved a late-night snack," Matt said.

"I'm standing by in the city lot on Wilson and Fourth," Hunter came back.

Matt nodded, then realized Hunter couldn't see him. "I copy. I'll let you know when they're on the move again. Hardy Two out."

"Roger. Hardy One out."

Matt adjusted his rear-view mirror so that it reflected part of the Grab-It Store. The large front windows allowed a peek inside the shop's brightly lit interior, stocked with shelves bulging with bags of different chips, cookies, cans of soup and vegetables, and mass-produced cupcakes. Milk, beer, and burritos jostled for space in the refrigerated cases.

Cole and Jesse stood at the cash register. They paid and walked out the door, Jesse dangling a plastic shopping bag from one hand, while Cole carried a couple of six-packs. The two climbed into the sedan. Its lights flashed on, then backed out.

With a start, Matt realized that the Black Sedan Boys might recognize his car since they had driven past it in the Babe-O-Licious parking lot. He punched the accelerator, rapidly pulling away from the curb but staying in the far right lane. He jerked his head back and forth between the windshield and his driver's door mirror as he endeavored to keep an eye on the sedan's headlights while trying not to crash into anything in front of him. That would be a conversation he didn't want to have with his mother.

His attention returned to the intersection barely in time to notice the traffic light blink to red. Matt jammed on the brakes, the radio and phone sliding to the floor. The black sedan moved into the left turn lane, and a van pulled up to his rear bumper. Another car stopped next to him. Matt reached for the walkie-talkie, but the lap belt prevented him from reaching it. The signal changed and the guy behind him honked. Matt waved an apology to the driver in the back of him and drove to the next corner, where he made a right and parked. He unbuckled himself and lunged for the handset.

"Hardy Two to Hardy One! Hardy Two to Hardy One!" Matt called into the mic.

"Hardy One. I copy."

"They just turned east on Foxglove. I couldn't follow because of traffic. I'm going to backtrack and try to pick them up. Over." Matt didn't wait for an answer, tossing the walkie-talkie on the passenger seat.

The radio ended speaker side down, the cushion muffling Hunter's voice. "I'm close by. I'm on my way. Hardy One out."

Matt wasn't planning to lose Cole and Jesse now. He reversed to Fourth and executed a wild left-hand turn, sweeping across all four lanes at once to skid around the Foxglove Street corner. The car wallowed through the turn, its body leaning like a sailboat into the wind. Matt planted the gas pedal to the floor, hitting sixty by the time he cleared the intersection. He slalomed between a bus and a slower truck before catching sight of the black sedan turning right on a side street. Braking hard, he followed at what he hoped was a discrete distance.

He ended up in an older residential neighborhood. The small homes with single-car garages looked like they were built in the 1940s. Most of the houses fronted well-tended gardens, although some yards seemed to serve primarily as storage spaces for old sofas and inoperative vehicles. Parked cars lined both sides of the pavement, and the large tree roots caused slabs of the sidewalk to jut up like miniature mountain ranges.

The single-family homes gradually gave way to apartment buildings. The black car entered the driveway of a two-story complex. It sported a newer, modern design, made of blocks and angles, painted gray with orange accents that seemed like an alien spaceship had landed in the area. Matt drove past it, finally parking in the lot of a small neighborhood park at the end of the next block. He killed his engine and doused the lights. He picked up the radio in one hand.

"Hardy Two to Hardy One," Matt said, "Hardy Two to Hardy One, come in, please."

"This is Hardy One. I copy."

"The Black Sedan Boys have gone back to their place. I'm at ..." Matt squinted his eyes to read the weakly lit wooden sign. "... Bushfall Park. Meet me here. Over."

"ETA four minutes. Hardy One out."

Matt put down the radio and glanced around the darkened rectangle of patchy grass nestled between the apartment buildings a little nervously, waiting for the friendly neighborhood serial killer clown to emerge from the undergrowth at any moment. A breeze caused the tree limbs to whisper, adding to the creep factor. He pushed the lock button, finding the thud of both doors latching comforting. Folding his arms, he sat back in his seat and stared into the middle distance. He jumped when somebody knocked on his window.

Hunter peered in.

Matt hadn't heard him arrive. He pulled on the handle, forgetting he had locked his car. Sheepishly, he hit the switch again, opened his door, and got out.

"They went into that gray apartment building down the block." The night was chilly, and Matt drew his arms close around him to stay warm.

"So, what do we do? Stake out where they live?" Hunter asked.

Matt shook his head. "No, but ... I only ... only it may be ... it ... I ..."

"A complete sentence, please."

"It is possible they're holding Trent in their apartment," Matt said. "At the Sleep Clinic, I didn't hear Sokolov say where they were taking him, so it could be there."

"That makes no sense. Why would the two of them hit a club and just leave their prisoner alone?" Hunter answered his own question. "Trent could be tied up and gagged." He shook his head. "No, he could still make noise."

"Or, perhaps a third person is involved, somebody we haven't met yet, or Sokolov is inside." Matt ran one hand through his hair. "That's stupid, strike that. His Highness is unlikely to volunteer for babysitting duty so his minions could go play at a strip club."

"Unless it is in their contract," Hunter deadpanned.

Matt remembered the hypodermic Sokolov threatened him with at the Sleep Clinic. "They could have drugged Trent. That would stop any noise problem." Matt punched a fist into his open hand. "Damn! If I could get a peek inside their apartment, I'd find out either if Trent is there or not." Matt sighed irritably. "And if I can't, I'd like to know their unit number. That's something, at least. Then the Black Sedan Boys wouldn't have won two nights in a row."

They were quiet for a moment. Hunter suddenly dashed to a park trashcan, fished an object out, and ran back to Matt.

"Here's our cover to wander around the complex this late." Hunter held up an empty delivery pizza box. "Somebody got the munchies. Hopefully, nobody gets close enough to smell it."

Matt grinned and gave Hunter a high five. "Let's go!"

The two drove to the apartments, parking their vehicles in the small visitors' lot in front. They climbed out of their cars and started toward a lit arch in the center of the building, Hunter holding the pizza box like a waiter with a tray.

"Stop skulking," Hunter whispered to Matt out of the corner of his mouth.

"I am not skulking!"

"You are too skulking. You look like you're planning a crime," Hunter said.

"I am," Matt returned, "breaking and entering."

"Well, don't be so obvious about it. Act as if you belong here," Hunter directed.

They reached the archway. Off to their left, a small alcove contained the complex's mailboxes.

"Let me check those." Hunter nodded toward the boxes and passed the box to Matt. Matt casually took it. Hunter cleared his throat and hinted firmly, "That pizza is hot."

"Oh." Matt held it level by two sides.

Hunter smiled. "Much better. I'll make an actor out of you yet." He darted into the alcove and returned almost immediately. "No names on them. Just the apartment numbers."

"We don't know the Black Sedan Boys' last names, anyway." Matt extended the box out to Hunter. "Careful, it's hot," he added.

Hunter took the carton back, quietly saying, "Ouch, ouch, ouch."

The two moved inside the complex. The apartments were arranged in a square surrounding a courtyard, and all the second-floor units were served by a common walkway. A swimming pool dominated the open space in the center, a light from beneath the surface casting odd, distorted shadows on the building. Lounge chairs lined up in neat rows along the deck. The only sounds came from the slapping of the water against the tiles.

Matt looked around at all the windows. He kept his voice low. "No lights on anywhere, so Cole and Jesse must be catching some Zs. No help there."

"Cars!" Hunter suggested. "Let's look in the parking lot. You know, spaces assigned to specific units. Find their car, check the number on the stall."

"Good idea!" Matt and Hunter hurried through another arch on the opposite side of the courtyard, emerging in a paved area behind the apartments.

The back of the building made up one side of the lot with small balconies on the second floor and fenced patios on the first. A cement block wall guarded the other three sides, unbroken except for the entrance and exit, which opened to a large driveway to the side. Cars filled most of the spaces.

Matt swore under his breath. None of the slots had any markings. "Foiled again," he muttered to himself sarcastically. He pointed to an arm gate next to the building, guarding the lot entrance. "Open parking. Tenants need a key card to get back here."

The black sedan sat in the far corner. Matt glanced at the dark windows puncturing the wall. Seeing no movement, he jogged to the car, Hunter behind him.

A small red light blinked on the dashboard. "An alarm," he said to himself.

"Of course it has one," Hunter said. "It's a pricey car."

"Do you have your phone?" Matt asked.

"Yes, but—"

"Make sure your ringer is on silent with vibration," Matt instructed. "I'm going to find a place where I can watch all the front doors without being seen. I'll send you a text when I do. When you get it, kick the car, jump on it, insult its mother, or do whatever you have to do to set off the alarm. Cole or Jesse will have to come out to reset it. I'll see which apartment they appear out of."

"Brilliant!" Hunter pulled out his phone and changed the settings. "Ready."

Matt ran back to the courtyard and crept to the top of the stairway to the first floor. The stairs continued to the roof, where a closed hatch blocked further access. His perch gave him a clear view of most of the upstairs and downstairs doors from here, or he could take a few long steps to the railing to check out the ones he couldn't see. He pulled out his phone and sent Hunter an empty text. Within a minute, the car alarm wailed. Matt suppressed a giggle. He was enjoying the game.

The door to the apartment next to the staircase opened. Matt backed up a few stairs into the shadows on the steps leading to the roof. Dressed only in a pair of sweatpants, Jesse hurried downstairs toward the parking area.

It was perfect luck! Matt hopped down to the common walkway to check the number on the Black Sedan Boys' apartment. The door stood ajar. Impulsively, Matt slipped in, softly shutting the door behind him.

A single lamp from a bedroom—Jesse's, Matt assumed—spilled out to illuminate the main room, comprising the kitchen, dining area, and living room. The apartment was stuffy, as though windows always remained shut, and smelled like unwashed gym socks. A heap of sporting equipment lay in one corner by the balcony sliding glass door. An old sofa, with a battered coffee table in front, sat across from a large screen television, the most expensive thing in sight. Football team posters and pin-ups of female cheerleaders in tight uniforms plastered the walls. Some dishes rested in a drainer on the kitchen counter, but more were piled in the sink.

Matt could see the dull gleam of a porcelain bathtub and toilet through the open door next to Jesse's room. To the left of the bathroom was another shut door, probably Cole's bedroom. Matt eased the door open. He thought he could detect faint snoring. Then he heard a soft thump and saw in the reflection of the dresser mirror Cole stirring under a messy pile of bedclothes. He gently closed the door.

He then realized how quiet it was. The alarm had been reset. He headed for the front door. Just as he was about to twist the knob, it rattled from the outside. Jesse groaned in exasperation from the other side and followed it with a pounding.

"Cole! Cole! I got locked out!" Jesse knocked on the door again. "Cole!"

An answering string of swear words came from Cole's room. Matt swiftly walked through the living room and slipped to the balcony through the glass slider, closing it behind him. He stuffed himself in the tiny amount of wall space next to the door and the railing. Cole, grumbling like a grouchy bear, shuffled to the front door and unlocked it. There was a brief, angry exchange between the roommates, then footsteps heading back to one bedroom. A second set came toward the sliding door. Matt glanced down: he hadn't shut it all the way. He pressed himself against the wall and sucked in his breath. Somebody inside slid the door completely closed and snapped the latch. In a minute, the light in Jesse's room switched off.

Matt tried the handle, even though logically, he knew he'd find it locked. It was. The only way out was by going down. He climbed over the banister and squatted down, gripping the iron banisters. He took a deep breath and lifted his feet off the balcony. Hanging vertically by his hands, he tightly wrapped his legs around one of the corner support posts below, like a fireman. He released the railing with one hand and hugged the post. He did the same with his other arm, working himself down the pole until he could rest his feet on top of a horizontal fence bar. He inched along until he leaped off to land safely on the asphalt below, then hurried back to the archway leading into the central courtyard. Hunter was waiting for him.

"They live in apartment 18. No Trent," Matt reported.

"Bad luck. But if my theater group ever performs Tarzan, you've got the part," Hunter said. "How do you look in a loincloth?"

"Stunning." Matt stared at the black sedan while an idea formed in his head. "How touchy was the car alarm?"

"Not very. I had to tug at the handle a couple of times to set it off," Hunter replied. "Why?"

"Run back to my car and bring me the roll of duct tape out of the trunk. Next to the tire jack," Matt said, eyes locked on the black sedan, tapping his index fingers to his lips. He held out his keys. "Quick, like a bunny."

Hunter took them and ran off. After another fast glance at the building's windows to check if the alarm had disturbed anybody, Matt jogged to the black sedan. Laying on his back, he wriggled beneath the car's trunk, examining the undercarriage. He located a likely spot under the rear bumper.

Hunter kneeled on the ground and looked under the car. "Got it."

Matt pulled his phone out of his pocket and checked the screen. "Good. Fully charged. Tear off a piece, about three inches or so."

He heard the tape being yanked off the roll. The sound abruptly stopped and was replaced by Hunter's quiet grunts as he tore a section off.

"Here." Hunter handed the adhesive to Matt.

"Thanks." Matt took it and secured his phone to the middle, leaving the two ends free.

"What are you doing?" Hunter asked.

"Later. Get ready to run if I set off the alarm. I have to be very careful." Matt took a deep breath. He remembered a game he played as a kid, where you had to remove silly things from a cartoon character with a pair of tweezers without setting off a buzzer. Now he played that in reverse. Gingerly, he positioned his phone into an open cavity on the bottom piece of the bumper and smoothed down the tape. "Let's go."

Matt slowly slid out from under the car, and the two walked back to their cars.

Hunter handed Matt his keys back. "What was all that about?"

Matt grinned. "Poor man's tracking device. I can follow the Black Sedan Boys by using the 'find my phone' app from my computer. All without leaving the comfort of my home!"

"Well played, sir, well played," Hunter congratulated.

"Now," Matt said, rubbing his hands together, "I'm hungry. How about going for a pizza?"

Chapter Twelve

MATT PUSHED AWAY FROM his computer with a groan, wondering if ever a CPU grew irritated at how many times it had been woken up so he could check the 'find my phone' website. It was almost sunset and the icon in the app hadn't budged from the map of the Black Sedan Boys' apartment building. He took another sip of coffee and leaned his head against the back of his chair, swiveling it side to side slightly. He wished Hunter could come over for company, but he'd received an email from his friend earlier that morning. Hunter's parents had handed him an ultimatum because he'd stayed out too late last night: perform a list of assorted chores or be grounded for the rest of his natural life. Hunter wisely chose the former.

Some roughness from the duct tape adhesive remained on the chair's arm. Matt rubbed it and briefly considered grabbing some rubbing alcohol to scour the stuff off. Might as well. It would give him something to do. Pushing himself up, he automatically glanced at his laptop.

The icon was in a different location.

Matt sat down and stared at the screen. He made himself count to twenty before he refreshed the app one more time.

The icon had moved again.

He wanted to text Hunter, so he reached for the spot he normally kept his phone before remembering it now rode with the black sedan. He could call Hunter from the landline extension in his parents' room, but he didn't want to leave his computer. Irrationally, he believed doing so would curse the entire program. Then he realized he hadn't memorized Hunter's number, and just added it to his phone's contacts list. He wondered if he also wrote it down some place.

Another look at the screen. The icon continued its movement. Antsy, Matt rose and walked around his room a few times. Too full of nervous energy to sit, he pulled his chair away from his desk and stood behind it.

The icon was on the highway leading out of town. Matt leaned on the back of his chair, puzzled. Where were they going? On vacation somewhere?

He had to pee. He held it as long as he could, then finally raced to the bathroom, returning in record time. The icon had traveled quite a distance from its last position. The car must be driving at a fast speed, he thought.

Matt rocked up and down on the balls of his feet. Excitement grew as he felt all the obstacles to finding Trent get blown aside.

The icon was now off the road, next to a gray rectangle on the map. Matt stared at the app. The diamond symbol remained in the same location. The car must have reached its destination.

Matt zoomed in on the map until the name of the splotch appeared. When he read it, he let out his breath in disbelief. "No way ..."

He snatched up his keys and raced out of his room.

The abandoned state mental hospital stood some distance from the city, surrounded by fields and vacant lots, alone, brooding, and defiant even as the housing developments crept ever closer. Built in the late 1800s, the gothic-styled design, complete with towers, cupolas, and arched windows, most likely intended to look reassuringly sturdy and safe, now more closely resembled a giant mausoleum. Ivy and weeds overgrew the immense structure, its bricks long ago losing their color from the pollution of the neighboring city and exposure to the weather. The second-floor balconies had collapsed, their windowpanes shattered, the frames and sills rotting with age.

Matt slowed on the two-lane rural highway as he drew along the decaying asylum. He checked to see if any other cars were nearby. It was clear, so he swung on the service road running next to the property. He turned off his headlights, leaving only his parking lights to guide him down the potholed and rough drive. The weeds grew so tall they brushed against the bottom of his car.

A high, wrought-iron fence surrounded the property. Matt bumped down the road until he reached a double gate. It was made of the same metal and just as high as the fence, flanked by two brick pillars. He braked to a stop and switched off his lights. The night engulfed him. After he shut off his engine, he realized how quiet the area was. There were no crickets, no leaves rustling in the breeze. The entire world held its breath, waiting.

Matt climbed out of his car, softly shutting the door, flashlight in one hand. He walked to the gate, the weeds swishing as he passed through. A metal plaque, embedded in the brick, proclaimed in overly ornate lettering 'Service Entrance'. A chain wrapped around the iron rungs, secured by a padlock that glinted in the beam from his flash. He saw why: the lock was shiny and new.

He examined it. The padlock had no markings that would show it was state property. Perhaps that was nothing, but he always thought the government tagged everything it owned. So somebody may have cut off the original padlock and substituted this one.

Matt flashed his light at the ground just beyond the gate. Two long, parallel rows, a few feet apart, pressed down the weeds as though flattened by car tires. As he looked closer, he noticed the marks left by the treads in the patches of soft earth running to an outbuilding's double doors. They were old, made of metal, and rusted around the edges, but another shiny padlock kept them shut.

Turning off his flashlight, Matt stepped back and scanned the fence. It stood at least eight feet tall, topped with spikes preventing anyone from scaling it. From either side, he thought as he recalled the building's function. He needed to find another way in.

The sound of a truck rumbling past on the highway made Matt recognize his car was still visible. If somebody—like a sheriff on patrol—would happen to look, they could spot it. He returned to the driver's seat and followed the road to the back of the asylum, which faced vacant land, bouncing and jostling over the uneven surface. A tree branch extended over the fence from the inside of the compound about halfway down. Although it hung about twelve feet above the ground, it might be possible to hoist himself into the tree and use the limb as a bridge to get onto the grounds. He needed a ladder, but he didn't have one handy until he realized he drove one.

Grinning, he maneuvered his car to the correct spot and turned off the engine. He picked up the flashlight, got out, and locked the door by habit. He felt a little silly about doing that as he slipped the flash into his pocket.

He scrambled on the car's roof and awkwardly hauled himself to straddle the limb, then up to a standing position. Gingerly, an apprentice tightrope walker, he inched along the branch over the fence, trying not to think about what would happen if he fell on the spear-like tips of iron below. He reached the trunk, climbed to the lowest limb, hung there for a second, then dropped to the ground. Brushing off his hands, he straightened up, more than a little proud of himself.

The acres of gardens surrounding the asylum still bore slight indications of the manicured grounds. Once-blooming flowerbeds and trimmed lawns stood neglected and overtaken by weeds and brambles. The stone pathways had cracked, the dirt had swallowed some, while an extra layer of grass covered others. He envisioned gaunt specters of the patients, strolling in the fresh air and healing sun, providing them with the illusion of normalcy for at least a short time.

Matt shook the vision from his head and decided to check the outbuilding to see if the black sedan was inside. If it was, maybe he could retrieve his phone as well.

He jogged over. Solid brick comprised the back and one side of the structure. He went around front and attempted to peek through the crack between the doors, but he saw nothing. The last wall contained a door and a few windows set too high for Matt to see through, even if he jumped. He rattled the doorknob. Locked, of course. Matt peered through the old-style keyhole, but all that met his eye was darkness. That meant he had to enter the old hospital blind, not knowing if the Black Sedan Boys were in residence or not.

The rear of the asylum appeared just as depressing and ominous as the front. The same rows of broken windows stared back at him, taunting him with their jagged edges. No illumination came from inside, although he half-expected, as per all good horror yarns, for a mysterious light to appear in the uppermost tower window.

He spotted a pair of double doors in the center of the ground floor. Crouching down, he headed for them, sprinting through the weeds and grass, dodging and weaving between overgrown bushes.

He reached the building and flattened himself against the wall next to the entrance. He didn't know why, but he had seen it in the movies. A thick layer of dust and cobwebs smothered the heavy wood doors. They sagged and hung a little open, only being held up by memory. The spiderwebs didn't cross the doorway, as though recently brushed away. He listened; no sound came from the interior.

Matt slowly slid over to one door, his shoes making a light scuffing noise against the dirt. He placed his palm against the door, rough and splintered under his hand. He pushed, expecting a soft creak, but the door issued a loud, fire-alarm-level shriek. Matt froze, holding his breath, waiting for the next shoe to drop: bats to come flapping out, the screeching of an angry cat, or a spectral, accented voice intoning 'Velcome'. After convincing himself none of those would occur, he stepped inside.

He stood in a narrow entry. Staircases flanked him on both sides, their metal railings shining dully from his flashlight. The stairwell reached the third floor. At the base of each set of steps, faded painted signs with arrows shaped like pointing fingers showed the way up to Wards A, B, and C. An illegible second sign pointed down the stairs that led to what had to be the basement.

If Sokolov held Trent here, Matt needed to search this place with some kind of system, otherwise, he could wander around this dreary place all night. He picked the left stairwell and started down. It was a brief trip: a sheet of plywood boarded up the passage just below floor level.

He trotted up the stairs and tried the set on the right. A wall blocked that one too, but it contained a door–with a new deadbolt. Matt ran his fingers over the smooth metal. A pick or a drill was required to open the lock, neither of which he carried with him, and he wasn't about to knock. Mentally noting the door for later investigation, he figured to check the rest of the asylum first.

Matt walked back to the central connecting corridor. It ran the entire length of the building, lined with doors. He thought conditions in the interior couldn't be any worse than the outside. He was wrong. Chunks of plaster that fell from the ceiling, exposing the lath behind, lay on the floorboards in heaps. The wood was dry and rotted in places, falling to the floor in jagged hunks. Paint, peeled in huge, irregular sheets, hung from the walls. The overall effect reminded Matt of being stuck inside a decomposing corpse.

The corridor was dark, the air thick with dust and the smell of mold and urine. Leaves, dirt, piles of plaster, and the occasional beer can littered the ground. Matt's footsteps crunched and echoed on the wooden floor as he walked, the sound bouncing off the walls and ceiling.

Start at the top and work your way down, he finally decided. He returned to the staircases and climbed the right one like a condemned man mounting the steps to the hangman's scaffold.

The third-story hallway appeared no different from the first, offering the same rubble of decay. He started down the corridor, his feet sinking into the thick layer of dust that coated the floor. He gasped when something ran over his foot: a rat. The rodent was huge, its body as big as his hand. He watched it scurry away, its long tail disappearing around a corner.

Matt peeked into the first room, the painted number 31 visible on the door. It was small, most likely for a patient. The remaining jagged slivers of glass in the window were so dirty that it was impossible to see through. The room's peeling paint probably had been a sterile white once, but now resembled the color of weak tea. A broken sink stood in a corner. The silent air still vibrated with sadness and desperation.

He continued to work his way around the floor, looking into each room. They didn't differ, except for the presence of a metal bed frame in one, a busted chair in another, and a wheelchair in a third. He wondered about the horrors of the past contained by this building, the madness of the patients who had occupied these cramped spaces. The hairs on the back of his neck started to tingle as a shiver crawled up his spine.

Returning to the stairs, he stopped before going down and became alert. For a second, it seemed a movement occurred somewhere else in the building. He didn't recall if he noticed a footfall, or perhaps a door closing, but he could have sworn he heard something. He stood still for a full minute, but nothing broke the deadly silence.

"Probably a rat," Matt said to himself.

He descended to the second-floor hallway. It was as depressing as the other two. With a sigh, he set off to check the rooms. He explored halfway down the right side when he sensed another mind entering his range. Before he could react, a man the size of a mountain rushed out of a room and tackled him.

The two crashed into the wall. The impact loosened some plaster, and it showered down on the struggling pair, white dust floating in the air. Matt squirmed, but the weight holding him down was too much and crushed him. Matt still held his flashlight, and he bashed it against his attacker's head a few times, grunting with each blow. The other weakened enough to let Matt wriggle out from under him. He scrambled to his feet, turned to flee, and faced Jesse.

Jesse blocked the hallway, crouched, arms wide, in a wrestling position. Behind Matt, Cole climbed to his feet, blood dripping down one side of his head from a gash on his temple. Matt's stomach lurched as Jesse rushed him.

Matt tried to dodge Jesse and make it back to the staircase. He grabbed the railing, but Jesse's hands clamped on his shoulders, the flashlight squirting out of Matt's hand. The beam spun through the air and disappeared into the dark over the edge, clattering as it hit the floor. He wiggled around; his back pressed against the banister. He flailed his arms, trying to push Jesse off, but the other was strong. Matt's legs kicked and his fists pummeled Jesse, to absolutely no effect. Only the grunts of their effort and the scuffling of their feet broke the silence. Matt squirmed and twisted, attempting to break free, but Jesse's grip was like iron. Finally, he brought his knee up into Jesse's groin, causing him to let go with a howl of pain. Matt scrambled away, and Jesse snatched for him, but Matt sidestepped too quickly, Jesse's fingers just brushing his shoulder. He fled down one set of stairs. Cole bounded down the opposite staircase, taking two steps at a time, and caught Matt at the landing.

The pair grappled in a desperate dance as they moved toward the window. Cole forced Matt backwards, pushing him through what glass and wood clung to the panes, the debris tinkling to the ground like discordant music. Matt's back hit the sill, and he bent backwards, head down. His legs kicked wildly, and his hands scrabbled at his attacker's clutches, but he couldn't break free.

Cole yanked Matt inside and threw him to the landing floor, jumping on top of him, Jesse adding his body to the dogpile. A confusion of arms and legs waved as all three combatants writhed on the wood like a ball of snakes until Cole got hold of Matt, picked him up, and pinned his arms behind his back.

"Hang on," Jesse got to his feet, panting, "that's the kid we took the jammer from."

"How very handy," Cole said. "Sokolov wants to talk with him. He's interested in you, for some reason, punk." Cole twisted Matt's arms higher up. "Anybody know you're out here?"

"No," Matt groaned out.

"How did he find us?" Jesse looked at Cole.

"Let's find out. How about it?" Cole increased the pressure.

Matt cried out and shook his head. Cole jerked Matt's arms up again.

"We shouldn't hurt him," Jesse warned in an anxious voice. "Sokolov would get mad."

Cole's chuckle was grim. "No need. That crazy Russian will pry the answer out of him, like he did with that other guy. I hope I get to watch. I want to hear you squeal like a pig, punk."

"What do we do with him until we talk with Sokolov?" Jesse asked.

"Stick this kid with the hypo. We brought it along," Cole said. "While he's out, we'll call the Russian."

Jesse pulled a box from one pocket and extracted a hypodermic. He pulled the protective cap off the needle. "We just grabbed this. How much do I give him?"

"What am I, a nurse? How the hell should I know?" Cole barked.

"But—" Jesse started.

"Look, I didn't bring the instruction folder with me! Empty the whole damn syringe into him! I'm getting tired of holding him!" Cole shouted.

Jesse injected the hypo into Matt's arm. Matt felt a sting as the needle punctured his skin, followed by the cold sensation of the liquid entering his body.

Jesse withdrew the hypodermic and stepped back. Cole released him.

Matt grasped the railing and steadied himself on his feet. He had a single thought: to get out of there. He had to. The voices of the others sounded like they came from inside a tunnel.

"Should I hold on to him?" Jesse held out his arms.

"Ah, don't bother," Cole said. "He ain't going to get too far with that stuff in him."

Matt's vision blurred. *I have to get out of here*, he told himself.

He inched sideways, hanging on the railing for support with two hands. He reached the stairs and looked down. They rippled like ocean waves. He stared down, using both feet one step at a time, a toddler learning to walk. His limbs tingled, and he rapidly grew exhausted, panting for breath. He stumbled and slipped down several steps, stopping his downward movement by clutching the banister. He breathed deeply for a few moments and resumed going downstairs, even though every part of his body urged him to give up and lay down.

The Black Sedan Boys nonchalantly followed him, Cole chuckling in derision. They weren't in a hurry; they didn't try to catch him. It was like they were walking a dog.

I have to get out of here ... I have to get out of here, Matt kept commanding himself.

Fog clouded Matt's brain. He reached the first floor and released the railing. He lost his coordination and staggered across the hall into the far wall. It required an effort to keep his head up and his eyes open. He shuffled toward the doors, arms hanging limp at his sides, leaning forward.

Suddenly, he sprawled on the ground. It disoriented him for a moment before he realized he had fallen. He raised up to his hands and knees and started crawling.

Out, he told himself, *just get out of the door.*

Cole and Jesse came up next to him. With a laugh, Cole put one foot on Matt's back and pressed down like he was squashing a bug.

Matt collapsed to the ground. His arms and legs moved uselessly. He was too tired to go any more. His muscles refused to respond. A swirling darkness poured in on him from all sides. He couldn't fight it off any longer. His body grew limp, and he tumbled to the void.

Chapter Thirteen

MATT'S EYES SNAPPED OPEN, but he could see nothing in the inky blackness. He blinked a few times, trying to adjust his vision, but it did no good. There was something in his mouth, a fuzzy material, and he tried to spit it out. He couldn't, then understood it was a gag.

Still groggy from the effects of the injection, his thinking refused to march in a straight line. His foggy brain forced him to take things one step at a time. He took a deep breath and a constricting pressure, like a leather belt running just below his chest, pushed back. Next, he twisted his wrists; two more straps secured them along his side. Working his way down his body, he discovered his ankles were also bound.

Another factor became apparent: he only wore his jeans and a metal surface, cold and hard, pressed against his bare back and heels. Then the puzzle completed: someone had securely strapped him down to a steel table of some sort.

He tugged at the restraints. They didn't give, but everything wobbled a little like it had wheels; maybe he lay on a gurney.

He was completely helpless. At least, the Black Sedan Boys didn't mummify him like the last time. Maybe he

should be thankful for their mercy, Matt thought sardon-
ically.

Matt wasn't sure how long he lived in a never-never land.
He shouted through the gag, hoping someone would hear
him, but his muffled voice only echoed back. Panic set in.
He wondered if they left him here to die, slowly, alone, and
in darkness, or had something worse in mind.

Immediately, all the gruesome killings he had ever
watched in horror movies over the years flooded back into
his mind: the victims screaming, the spurting blood, the
sickening thud of the bodies hitting the ground. Now he
was sorry he had viewed them. His heart raced, and a cold
sweat beaded on his forehead.

No, no; he willed himself not to consider that possibility.
That made little sense. Cole or Jesse could have simply
thrown Matt out of the window during the fight. Those
two simple minds couldn't concoct this elaborate setup,
although they had come up with a duct tape trick at his
house. He had to give them props for that one. But now,
time for him to think about his current location.

He didn't know if he was still in the mental hospital or
if they had transported him somewhere else while unconscious. He listened. All he could hear was his own
breathing. He sniffed the air. It smelled of the same musty
odor from the asylum hallways, so he must still be in the
same building. After the Black Sedan Boys injected him
with the anesthetic, they must have brought him to this
room, stripped him down, and strapped him to the gurney.
But in preparation for what?

The drug still lingered in his system, and Matt got drowsy
again. His eyelids grew heavy as he fought to keep them

open, but he didn't win, and soon his eyes closed as he dozed off. The world around him faded until darkness surrounded him. He lost track of time while drifting in and out of sleep.

A sound jolted him awake: the coughing, sputtering, and finally starting of a small engine, soon joined by a second one, in a room next door. Above him, an LED light flickered to life. It throbbed like a heartbeat, in time to the chugging of the generator, until blossoming to full, glaring brightness, hurting his eyes. The bulb was taped to a large, circular pale blue metal fixture made up of more round, non-working lights, making Matt feel as though he were being stared at by the multi-part eye of a giant bug. He then recognized it as the type of light used in operating theaters.

Matt looked around. He lay on the gurney with enough space to move around the room. Blue tiles, cracked and dirty, lined the walls. Drilled holes marked the position where equipment had once been mounted. To his right, a folding table held a laptop, as well as two other instruments. He didn't know their function. Although the table was old and dented, the computer and the devices appeared new. A door opened and closed behind him. Footsteps approached.

Matt shivered as Sokolov appeared by the side of the table, his hands clasped in front of him. The addition of wearing a lab coat made him appear like a young intern. He stared down at Matt with all the empathy of a biologist looking at a slide of pond scum under a microscope. The graduate assistant pulled a flashlight from his breast pocket and leaned over the gurney. With his thumb and index finger, he spread open each of Matt's eyes, shining the light

into them, and examining them. He straightened up, his
face set in a mask of concentration, his brow furrowed in
thought.

"They administered a larger dose of the anesthetic than
usual," Sokolov said to Matt in a perfunctory tone as he
walked over to the table. "That was an error. There may
be some aftereffects." He came back to the gurney after
picking up a small tube. "It was the same drug I tried to inject you with at the Sleep Clinic. I congratulate you on the
adroit trick you pulled, by the way. I spent the entire Open
House asleep. Given how much I dislike those, however,
not that much of a loss."

He squirted two globs of a thick, sticky gel on each side
of Matt's chest. The goop was cold and made his skin
crawl. Sokolov replaced the tube on the table and picked
up two sensors attached to long wires. He wiggled them in
the gel, then walked back to the equipment, saying, "This
is a cardiac monitor, only for the rate." He flipped the
switch on one instrument and a soft ping, sounding like a
metronome, beat in time with Matt's heart. Sokolov stared
at the readout for a moment before returning to Matt's
side.

"Now look on the floor to your left. You will observe an
electrical cable running from this table to an opening in
the wall. Do you see it?" Sokolov curtly asked.

Matt turned his head to his right and spotted the cord.

"Do you see it?" Sokolov demanded.

Matt nodded.

"It connects one end to a generator in the next room
with this gurney. I'm sure you remember your elementary
school science and what conducts electricity." Sokolov

knocked on the metal table's surface. "While discredited for psychological experiments as well as treatment for mental health issues, electric shock has benefits. Compliance, for one. After I remove the gag, I expect complete and total cooperation, or you will suffer the consequences. Do you understand my meaning?" His tone was low and menacing, his eyes cold and hard.

Matt nodded, his throat dry.

Sokolov reached for the gag and pulled it off. Matt gasped for air and spat out some fibers left in his mouth. "Does anybody else know you are here?"

"No."

"That is fortunate for you. We begin." He returned to the laptop. "Name?"

"Matt Storm." His voice sounded small in the room. It sounded tinny and far away when it echoed off the walls.

He tapped in the information. "Age? In years and months."

"Seventeen years, two months."

The clicking of the keyboard loomed loud and ominous in the quiet room. It was the only sound besides the beep-beep-beep of the heart monitor. "Height and weight?"

"Six feet exactly. 142 pounds."

"How old were you when you discovered you were telepathic?" The question came like asking how many sugars for coffee. There was no inflection, no emotion.

"Dude, you've gotten hold of some misinformation. I'm not tel—" Matt began.

A surge of electricity coursed through him. He screamed as his back arched off the table, and the shock wave sizzled through his body, setting every nerve ablaze. It was like a million tiny needles piercing his skin simultaneously. His heart raced, and the beeping from the monitor turned staccato. Then, as suddenly as it had started, it ended. He slumped down on the table, covered in sweat, every inch of his body tingling.

"You said shock, not electrocution," Matt gasped out.

"I have no control over the intensity. Merely if the current is on or not. Now, no more games." Sokolov's voice turned deadly quiet. "Or would you prefer a longer jolt?"

"No ... no ... not that." Matt swallowed some drool in his mouth, while more ran down his chin. "What was the question again?"

"How old were you when you discovered you were telepathic?" Sokolov repeated.

"Eight, about eight years old," Matt said, trying to catch his breath.

"Anybody else in your family have this skill?" Sokolov's fingers poised above the keyboard.

"No," Matt added, "At least, not that I know about." He risked a question. "How did you find out?"

A proud smile turned up Sokolov's lips. "Your eye coloring. It is very unusual, and the same as Subject T.S."

"Subject T.S.?" Matt asked with a hint of sarcasm. His eyes narrowed, and he cocked his head to the side. "You mean Trent, don't you?"

Sokolov ignored him. His eyes glittered with something that looked like excitement. "I noticed their color that day when you returned the drive to the Sleep Clinic. It reminded me of Subject T.S."

"Trent. His name is Trent."

Sokolov paid no attention to his remark. "I think you noticed my curiosity and cleverly prevented me from taking a closer look. I couldn't be absolutely sure about my observation or my hypothesis, though. When I viewed the photos my subordinates took of you during their visit to your house, I was almost positive I was correct. Subject T.S. confirmed my hunch recently."

Matt went cold as he imagined how Sokolov got that 'confirmation'. "You forced Trent to tell you."

"Persuaded," Sokolov's voice was soft, but with a knife-like edge that made Matt uneasy, "Now we will obtain a baseline measurement. I will use an EEG." He patted the instrument with pride. "It's an older unit, but I have modified it to meet my needs. You see, your skill generates unusual brain waves. I wish to determine if it is the same as Subject T.S.'s pattern."

Sokolov picked up something which resembled a swimming cap, but with several leads running out. He fed out the wires, being careful not to snag or pull them, and then slipped the cap on Matt's head. The sensors inside felt like ice against his scalp. Sokolov returned to the EEG and flipped a switch.

As soon as he did, Matt was no longer in the room. Instead, his mind escaped his skull, traveled down the wires embedded in the cap, and crossed into a different universe. Just like his experience with his own laptop, he seemed to transform into a non-physical being made from no substance. He was nothing but thought and energy, floating in a vast sea of colors. He could sense the lights and power bursting in every direction; they melded into a huge rainbow spectrum, pulsing and burning like bonfires.

Color saturated his mind. Blue and green spread apart like fireworks. Nestled in each colorful explosion, he sensed, lay the EEG, the heart monitor, and the laptop. The only exception to the beauty was a black hole that must represent Sokolov. Another mind appeared in the swirling hues. Matt concentrated.

Trent? Is that you?

Matt! Where are you?

I'm here in—

An electric shock snapped Matt back into the operating theater. His muscles spasmed, and his face contorted with pain. He couldn't stop the screams that ripped from his throat. The cadence of beeps from the heart monitor increased. The power shut off, and Matt's body relaxed again. He opened his eyes, finding himself staring into the overhead LED light once more.

"Are you listening to me?" Sokolov was saying.

"You sound like my parents," Matt muttered. He was aware of that other world, beckoning just beyond his consciousness, like a beautiful spring day outside of his classroom window. It was difficult not to get drawn back to it. "Yes, yes, I am."

"Excellent." Sokolov picked up a deck of cards and continued as though a visiting college lecturer. "These are Zenner cards, designed by psychologist Zenner for use by his colleague, J.B. Rhine, in the study of extra-sensory perception."

"Will there be a test later?"

Sokolov shot an angry glance at Matt. He resumed his professional delivery as he held the deck up and fanned it open. "As you can see, it comprises twenty-five cards with five unique designs: circle, square, star, cross, and wavy lines." He shuffled the deck. "When I look at one card at a time, you tell me which one it is."

"Before your trigger finger becomes itchy there, Tex, you're too far away. I can't read you from where you're standing," Matt said.

"Really? Distance is a factor? That is fascinating. I never considered that." Sokolov typed some notes into the laptop. "How far? In feet and inches."

"You have to be two or three feet away from me." Sokolov started to move, hesitated, and Matt blurted out, "Look, bro, I'm strapped to a table. I can't do anything, even though I want to pound your face in. And no, I can't perform any Jedi mind control tricks, either."

Sokolov walked closer wearily. Matt shuddered when he came into contact with that reptilian consciousness. After receiving Matt's confirming nod, the graduate assistant picked up the top card from the deck and looked at it.

"What card—" he started.

"Circle. You've noticed there's a stain on it. Coffee, probably. You really ought to be more careful."

"Interesting." Sokolov slipped the first card under the bottom of the deck and selected the next one down.

"Cross. No stain on that one."

Sokolov flipped to the next card, and the next, with Matt naming each one in a bored voice, until he completed the entire set. Sokolov returned to his laptop. "One hundred percent accuracy. Very impressive."

"Why, I'm so very glad you think so," Matt mocked.

The longest electrical jolt yet surged through Matt. He strained against the restraints, his muscles bulging and straining, the leather cutting into his skin. He screamed, and the taste of metal filled his mouth. The beeps from the heart monitor sounded like a machine gun. The current cut off. Matt collapsed back to the gurney, his body twitching and sweaty. The flavor of blood remained, and his head pounded. It felt like a truck had hit him.

Sokolov leaned on the table and loomed over Matt. "The next time we meet, I could do without the snark. Remember that." He straightened up and flashed a wintry smile. "I'm sure I'm sounding like your parents again."

Without saying another word, Sokolov lifted the cap from Matt's head and unstrapped the leads and electrodes. He replaced the equipment on the table and switched everything off. The heart monitor ping stopped, and a velvety quiet draped the room. Sokolov turned toward the laptop, his fingers clicking across the keys as he typed in a few more lines of notes. He put down the lid of the computer and left the room, not paying any more attention to Matt, as though he had turned into another piece of furniture.

"See ya around!" Matt called out as the door shut behind Sokolov.

He closed his eyes and tried to find Trent's mind again. Nothing. What happened? Why could he contact Trent a few minutes ago, but not now? He breathed out an irritated growl and looked toward the table.

That was it! He reasoned, *The equipment! That must be the difference.*

Matt used self-hypnosis with his laptop, but not this time. He had only entered the—he didn't know what to call it—alternate dimension, thoughtscape, whatever, when the EEG powered up. It connected to the laptop, and the laptop was likely hooked to the internet via a cellular signal. Sokolov was proud that he had modified the EEG. Accidentally, he'd also created a setup that broadcast Matt and Trent's brainwaves to each other. The first time Trent called out to him, at Hunter's house, he must have been hooked up to the EEG. Matt shivered as he understood why Trent was screaming.

The Black Sedan Boys came up to the gurney. Jesse had something folded over one arm.

Cole released the straps over Matt's chest and wrists. "Sit up and hold your arms in front of you."

Matt had no choice but to obey as Jesse snapped the filthy white canvas garment open. It was a jacket with three buckled straps across the chest and two long sleeves with a ring of fabric at the ends.

A straitjacket.

Cole grabbed Matt's forearms as Jesse slid Matt's arms into the garment. Matt struggled to resist, but he was no match against the combined strength of the other two. Cole crossed the sleeves of the jacket to trap Matt's arms against his chest, the cloth coarse and abrasive. The buckles were fastened so that the straps pulled the jacket tight against Matt's body. He could not move his arms.

Jesse loosened Matt's ankles. "Get off."

Matt swung his legs off the gurney and hopped to the ground. Cole started walking toward the door; it was obvious that Matt was to follow, with Jesse bringing up the rear. They stepped into a hallway. A square of light streamed out from behind them, but darkness lay beyond. There were no windows, so they must be in the asylum's basement.

Cole switched on a flashlight, splitting the shadowy grayness with a cone of light. It was a corridor in the same condition as the others Matt had seen: plaster and debris on the floor, peeling institutional gray paint, wires hanging from the ceiling where once hung lighting fixtures. Unlike the straight upstairs hallways, though, the basement resembled a haunted house maze.

They started walking, the Black Sedan Boys' shoes crunching along the dirty floor, Matt feeling the grit and dirt under his bare feet. Making a left turn, the group ended up in a shorter, dead end hallway, lined by a few doors, featureless other than a small, square window at eye level. Matt spotted the padlocks on doors across from each other. They stopped in front of one.

Cole wedged the flashlight between his elbow and ribs. He wiggled a key into the lock, and it clicked. He pushed on the door with one foot. Dust motes danced in the beam of light that he swung around the walls of the small room, perhaps six feet square. The remnants of padding, shredded and dangling like loose skin and blackened by time, lined the walls.

Matt took a step back. "No, not in there," he said, his voice pleading. "Please, anywhere else. I don't like small spaces. Strap me back on the table, but don't make me go in there."

"You're making me cry," Cole sneered. He shoved Matt into the room so hard that he collided with the far wall. The door closed, the lock snapping shut.

The Black Sedan Boys left, their footsteps fading along with the light.

Matt stood in the center of the unlit room, trembling at the close tightness. So here he was in a padded cell wearing a straitjacket.

He figured he'd end up in one, eventually.

Chapter Fourteen

MATT HAD NEVER BEEN claustrophobic, he reminded himself, merely uncomfortable in tight spaces. He refused to consider the term 'claustrophobia'. It was just another label he didn't need, even if it maybe was true. Yet the room felt so close, and his anxiety built. He stood still, mentally pushing against the walls that tried to crush him. He ordered them to return to their expected places, to leave him alone.

A voice whispered in the darkness, "Matt?"

Matt started. "Trent? Trent, where are you? Are you in here with me?"

"Keep it down! Don't let them hear you!" Trent hissed. "I'm in the room across the hall."

"Wait! Let me get to the window." Matt stepped forward and hit a wall. Putting his right shoulder against it, he walked ahead, turned one corner, and barked his shin against what must be a toilet bowl. He rounded another corner, then finally rubbed the door frame. He faced forward and shuffled sideways until he sensed the opening. "Okay. Set. I'm out of range. Are you?"

"Yes, but didn't I communicate with you a short time ago? How did that happen?"

Matt told Trent his theory about Sokolov's modified EEG.

"Makes sense. Now, though, we're going to have to talk the old-fashioned way, like you wanted when we met that first day," Trent replied. "How did you end up here? What are you doing here?"

"I came to rescue you," Matt answered. "I don't know if the irony carries in the dark."

Trent chuckled. "Loud and clear. How did you find me?"

"I used my phone to track the two goons. I planted it in their car," Matt said, "hoping that they would lead me to where you were being held. It did, but before I could do anything about it, Cole and Jesse jumped me. Those two don't mess around."

"No, they don't," Trent agreed.

"Who are those guys? Do you know?"

"They used to be football players at the university," Trent explained. "Cole's basically a bully, and on the field, it was allowed, even encouraged. He was so rough there was some talk that if Cole didn't make it as a pro player, he had a job waiting for him in the Mafia. They both got caught in a sex scandal with two cheerleaders. Allegations flew of what the administration delicately termed 'sexual misconduct'. Anyway, they were kicked out. Sokolov pays them, of course, but he also promised to have them readmitted and reinstated on the football team." The darkness was silent for a moment. Trent went on, his voice low and subdued, "I'm sorry I brought you into this, Matt. I should have just hiked past you in the woods that day. But like you said, how could I pass up a chance to meet another telepath? I resisted telling them about you for as long as possible, but ..." he trailed off.

"Don't blame yourself, Trent," Matt dropped into a sarcastic, fake German accent, "he has ways of making people talk."

"I know from experience. From hearing your screams, so do you."

"Amen to that, brother. How did he learn about telepathy?" Matt asked. "At least at first?"

"I told him," Trent confessed.

"You told him!"

"Keep it down!" Trent was quiet for a while, then he continued, "In my freshman psych course, we could earn extra credit if we volunteered for various studies. I mean, that's how all the professors got their subjects. I signed up for one at the Sleep Clinic, under Dr. Richter. Sokolov was his graduate assistant. He ran the actual study; Dr. Richter just reviewed the reports and conferred with Sokolov."

"You don't think Richter is involved?"

"No. He's a nice guy. Very respected in his field, a big shot," Trent said. "Sokolov noted some abnormalities in my EEG and asked if I knew about them. I jokingly replied I did, because I read minds. Remember, I told you where I came from? It made no waves there."

"Yes."

"Sokolov didn't react at first, then later claimed Dr. Richter was conducting different research during the summer, a ground-breaking study on higher brain functions such as ESP," Trent went on, "and he wanted me to take part. He would pay me a stipend, and I would receive free housing. It flattered me that somebody as important as Dr. Richter asked for my help, so I agreed."

"Didn't you read in Sokolov's mind that he'd lied?" Matt responded with some irritation.

"He made the offer over the phone," Trent answered. "And every time I met with Sokolov at the Clinic, I found him as cold and distant as you most likely have. But he can also be incredibly charming, both in person and in his thoughts when it suits him. One day, though, I couldn't read him at all. I mentioned it, and he proudly displayed his jammer. He switched it off as part of his demonstration, and that slip allowed me a glimpse into his mind, into his true self, and how he only uses people. I figured out what I was told about the experiment's goals was false, and I told him so. We argued, and I left. Before I did, I moved some data files to a USB drive and deleted the originals from his computer. I even swiped the jammer. Sokolov sent Cole and Jesse after me, but I took off into the forest to escape them. I thought I had, but they caught me at the restaurant, jabbed a syringe into me, and hustled me to their car before I passed out."

"What does that guy want from us? To learn how to be telepathic?"

"I have no idea. He never thought about his exact plans, but whatever they are, I don't think they're good," Trent said.

"What do we do now?" Matt tried not to sound as hopeless as what weighed him down.

"We have no choice. We have to cooperate for the present," Trent said. "But we're like prisoners of war. We have to keep an eye open for escape. One thing is for sure. If one of us gets a chance, he needs to make a break for it. Alone, if need be. Leave the other and go for help."

"Trent, I'm not going—" Matt tried to object.

"No arguments," Trent interrupted, "If we both can't go, I leave you, and you leave me. Agreed?"

"No!"

"This isn't the time for heroics or nobility, Matt. We don't have the luxury," Trent said firmly.

"But—"

"Matt!" Trent snapped. "Agreed?"

Matt sighed. "Agreed. Under protest."

"Noted for the record." Trent shushed Matt. "They're coming."

The flashlight beam bounced up the hallway, splitting into the darkness. Matt instinctively backed into the room. Cole and Jesse stopped outside the doors.

"Feeding time at the zoo!" Cole laughed. A sack was shoved through the window on the door. It rustled as it dropped to the floor. "Chicken sandwich and fries!"

"How am I supposed to eat when I'm trussed up like this?" Matt protested.

"Off the ground, like a dog," Cole sneered.

"At least a dog has four legs!" Matt shot back.

"He's right, Cole," Jesse said a little tentatively, appearing nervous of Cole's reaction. "Let him loose. It's not like he can go anywhere. Not in there."

"Oh, okay, okay," Cole grumbled. He poked the flashlight through the window, blinding Matt. "You, Fido. Find a corner and turn your back to the door."

Matt did so. The padlock was unlatched and the door swung open. Jesse came up behind Matt and started undoing the buckles.

"Just a second," Jesse said. "Be cool."

"Yeah, chill, man. I won't give you any trouble," Matt said. It surprised him to read sympathy in Jesse's mind.

Jesse released the straps. "Turn around."

Matt faced Jesse, sighing with relief as he removed the straitjacket. "Thanks, dude, I appreciate it."

Jesse picked up the sack of food and handed it to Matt. "Is it true?" he spoke quietly, "what they say you can do?"

"Yes." For a second, Matt read a thought darting through Jesse's mind. He said softly, "You fear Cole, don't you?"

"Why not spoon-feed him, too, like a baby?" Cole's sarcastic question bulldozed into the room from the hallway.

Jesse shoved the bag into Matt's hand. "Here," Jesse said harshly, "don't choke on it."

Cole and Jesse, Cole chuckling at Jesse's remark, left the cell, the padlock clicking behind them. Another sack plopped through the window in Trent's door, but he couldn't hear anyone laughing or talking. The glow of their flashlight faded down the hall, and their footsteps eventually disappeared.

Matt sat, the bag beside him. He began to open the sack normally, but suddenly ripped into it and shredded the paper across the floor. He tore into the wrapper and threw it to the ground, devouring the sandwich, then jammed the fries into his mouth and chewed like a starving animal. After he finished, he felt around the floor for any morsel he might have spilled. Not finding any, he moved to sit in a corner. *Like the dog I am*, he thought.

The next thing Matt was aware of was something pushing into his side. He opened his eyes; he hadn't remembered dropping off.

"Wake up, Sleeping Beauty." Cole dug the toe of his boot into Matt's stomach. He held the straitjacket. Jesse hung by the open door. "Get up. The head guy wants you."

Matt got up and obediently put out his arms. "No trouble."

"You're getting smart." Cole secured Matt in the straitjacket and motioned toward the hallway.

Matt went into the hall, noticing that Trevor's door was also unlocked. The two walked down the corridor without talking, their feet making soft crunching sounds against the dirt on the floor. He squinted a little at the bright light in the operating room as he stepped inside.

Trent lay strapped to the gurney, already hooked up to the heart monitor and EEG. He and Matt exchanged sick smiles that were as much out of anticipation as dread. Matt realized he couldn't read Trent's thoughts, even though he was in range. Trent must have noticed Matt's puzzled look and figured out that something was amiss. He looked at the equipment table. Matt followed Trent's gaze and saw the jammer sitting there, apparently working just fine.

Sokolov stood by his laptop, dressed again in his lab coat, entering some data. He ignored everybody else until he finished typing. At last, he turned and addressed Trent, "Subject M.S. stated you have a functioning range for your skills."

"We're people, we have names, we're not laboratory animals!" Matt shouted. At the same time, he moved to the gurney.

"That could be argued," Sokolov coolly responded. "Well, Subject T.S.? What is your distance?"

Matt tapped his foot twice against a table leg. He hoped Trent would pick up on the message.

"Two, about two feet." Trent and Matt exchanged looks.

Matt gave an inside sigh of relief.

"Why didn't you mention that fact before, Subject T.S.?" Sokolov demanded.

"You never asked." Trent flashed a sweet smile.

The Black Sedan Boys snickered, and Sokolov glared at them. "Once you've finished enjoying your little joke, set up the experiment."

Jesse stepped out of the room, returning with a metal folding chair, a card table, and a leather strap. Cole took the chair and placed it two feet from the gurney. He squatted down and retrieved from under the gurney two thick electrical cables which had large alligator clips at each end; it looked like a car jump starter. He clamped the set between a gurney leg and the chair, then stood.

Sokolov pointed to Matt. "He needs his hands free."

Cole removed Matt's straitjacket. "Sit down."

Matt did so. Cole took the strap and secured Matt to the chair with it, a seat belt buckled in the rear. Jesse moved in, unfolding the legs of the card table. He placed it on the ground in front of Matt, then scooted it in, right against Matt's middle.

"Forearms on the table at all times," Sokolov directed. Matt rested his arms on the tabletop, palms down. Sokolov dismissed the Black Sedan Boys with a wave of a hand. "Wait outside."

Cole and Jesse nodded, stepping into the hall and closing the door.

Sokolov faced Matt and Trent. "Before we begin today's work, I remind you we attached the gurney and chair to the generator. I expect compliance. If one of you doesn't, you will both receive the consequence. Is that clear? Give me a verbal response. Subject T.S.?"

"Yes," Trent said.

"Subject M.S.?"

"Yes," Matt answered.

"Now that we have that understood, we shall proceed. This ought to be interesting. I haven't recorded the brainwaves of a sender yet, just the ones from the receiver. I wonder if there will be any difference," Sokolov said. "In the 1970s, United States intelligence agencies and their Soviet Union counterparts reportedly tried experiments with what they termed 'remote viewing'. That was the ability of people with claimed psychic abilities to see and describe a remote location. A form of long-distance espionage, if you like."

"Oh, goodie, another lecture," Matt muttered under his breath.

Sokolov shot Matt a scathing look and continued, "From the declassified results released to the public, those attempts failed completely. Perhaps they overestimated the distance telepathy could travel."

"By a few hundred miles," Trent added.

"Our experiments so far—" Sokolov began.

"Our?" Matt snorted.

"Our experiments so far have been relatively simple, communicating basic geometric shapes," Sokolov pushed on. "Now, we move on to a different level. Our next experiment involves a slightly more complicated message." He placed a stack of cards on the table in front of Matt. "You, of course, recognize the Zenner cards." Sokolov paused as though waiting for a response.

Matt nodded.

He continued, "However, note that the symbols are colored. Red squares, blue squares, and so forth."

"Did your goons color them in for you in their free time?" Matt asked. He thought he perceived the faintest trace of a smile on Sokolov's face at his description of the Black Sedan Boys.

"No, I used psych student interns. They at least stay inside the lines," Sokolov commented dryly. He pointed toward Trent. "Next to Subject T.S. is a small screen. It will display various patterns constructed with those cards. He will telepathically transmit those designs to you, Subject M.S. You will then duplicate them on the tabletop, using the deck in front of you." Sokolov returned to his laptop. "The interns have already performed this task, verbally, of course, so I know how long each one should take to complete. If your performance is slower, I will assume you are not attending and are communicating on different matters. You both will receive a consequence. Are the instructions clear?"

"Yes," Matt and Trent replied.

Sokolov switched on the EEG, and Matt immediately sensed Trent's mind, but his thoughts were distant and hidden behind the interference. It didn't seem to matter whether the EEG provided any boost to telepathy. The jammer blocked any signals.

"Turn off the jammer," Matt requested.

"Oh, yes, I forgot." Sokolov turned off the device.

Trent's thoughts blasted into Matt's head: *All right Matt, let's show this jackas—*

"Began now," Sokolov ordered. "The first image is on the screen."

Ready, Trent. Matt concentrated just on Trent's thoughts, ignoring everything else.

It's a square design, three by three. Upper left-hand corner: blue cross.

Matt searched through the cards, found the correct one, and placed it on the table. *Got it. Next?*

Red triangle in middle. Yellow star on right.

The two worked efficiently, quickly finishing pattern after pattern. A smug, self-satisfied smile grew on Sokolov's face as he watched, as though he were performing all the work. Finally, the experiment was over.

"Excellent!" enthused Sokolov. "Perfect accuracy!"

Matt opened his mouth to say something smart but remembered the electrical jolt the last time he did. He remained quiet, soon hearing a communication from Trent.

Matt, remember to—

Sokolov switched the EEG off and turned on the jammer. Trent's thoughts vanished. Matt couldn't read anything. He'd always wanted that to happen, and now that it had, he wasn't happy about it. It surprised him. He didn't like it and felt oddly lonely.

"Boys!" Sokolov called. When Cole entered, Sokolov pointed to Matt. "I'm finished with Subject M.S. I have further work I wish to perform with Subject T.S."

Cole walked over to Matt and pulled the table away. He undid the belt, then jerked his head toward the door. "You heard him, mental marvel. Out."

Matt stood and shuffled out of the room, giving a thumbs-up to Trent as he passed. He stopped in the hall, Cole stepping in front of him. He held up the straitjacket.

"Must we go through that again?" Matt sighed.

"Yes, we must go through that again," Cole mimicked.

Matt rolled his eyes and extended his arms. Time froze. If Matt had seen the situation in a movie, he wouldn't have believed it, but here it was, etched razor sharp: Jesse was on one knee behind Cole, tying his shoelaces. Cole stood, holding the straitjacket in front of him. The cosmos had just sent him an open invitation. It would be rude not to accept.

It had all happened in seconds. Matt shot forward, shoving Cole, causing him to tumble over Jesse's back. Turning, Matt darted down the corridor toward the faded EXIT sign.

He slid around a corner in a skidding turn, his arms splayed out, flapping to keep his balance. Matt reached the bottom of the stairs. Bounding up the steps two at a time, he twisted the lock and threw open the door.

He ran up to the entry and rushed through the double doors, flinging them wide. He cried out in pain as he stepped outdoors. The ground was rough and uneven, full of sharp rocks and stones. Every bump and shard pressed into the soles of his bare feet. He moved forward as fast as he could, wincing repeatedly. He might as well be treading over cut glass.

Cole's voice came from behind him. "Stop! Stop!"

Mercifully, Matt reached a section of the grounds that was once been a lawn. He hoped the tall grass and weeds didn't hide a broken bottle or other sharp, unpleasant surprises as he sprinted toward the tree. Out of the corner of his eyes, he saw Cole and Jesse split up, approaching him from either side.

A game of keep away began. Matt dodged and weaved as the Black Sedan Boys came at him from every angle, football players closing in on the quarterback. Jesse grabbed his arm, but Matt yanked away. Cole blocked the path to the tree. Matt veered toward the fence instead. He put on a burst of speed, ignoring the pain from every rock, stone, or pebble he stepped on. Matt's feet stung, but he kept going until he reached the fence. It seemed as if it had grown five feet taller since he saw it the first time.

He grasped two iron uprights. He logically knew he couldn't climb the fence; that was as impossible now as when he first arrived. Still, he had to try. It was his only option. Maybe he could jump high enough to reach the top railing. Maybe he would be saved by adrenaline, which he had always heard was released during accidents to allow people to perform superhuman feats. It could be true, he reasoned. Could be.

Hands grabbed him, yanking him back. He stretched out his arms, his fingers desperately trying to grasp the fence again, almost like a shipwreck victim clutching for the last remaining lifeboat. Jesse pinned his arms behind him. Matt struggled but was caught in a vise.

Cole staked out the ground in front of him. "Nobody makes a fool of me," he growled. His fist drove into Matt's stomach.

Matt cried out.

"Sokolov doesn't want him hurt," came a worried caution from Jesse.

"He won't see the damage," Cole snarled back.

Cole continued punching. Matt groaned at every hit landing on his midsection, his body growing more and more numb with each one. A look of triumph and pleasure glowed in Cole's eyes.

"Hey, bro, stop, hold it," Jesse said. "Too much, man, too much."

Cole delivered a final blow to Matt's gut, then stepped away, shaking one hand as though it were sore.

Jesse released Matt, and with a moan, he slumped to the ground.

"All right. Let's take him back inside."

Chapter Fifteen

JESSE ESCORTED MATT DOWN the dirty corridor again. He still wore the straitjacket, but it seemed looser than before. The Black Sedan Boys dumped Matt back in the padded cell after the beating, and it wasn't until Jesse came to get him later that Matt didn't know if he had passed out, fallen asleep, or just stopped caring.

By the time he'd snapped out of it, he had the straitjacket on once more.

"You shouldn't have pulled that stunt," Jesse told Matt.

"Prisoners have the duty to escape, don't they?" Matt didn't wait for an answer. "Well, so do lab rats."

"How do you feel?" Jesse asked.

"My ribs are still sore."

"You're lucky he didn't break them."

Matt looked Jesse in the eyes. "Thanks for calling Cole off, man. I owe you."

Jesse grunted a reply.

The two walked in silence. Matt cast a sidelong glance at Jesse. He figured he was the weakest link and made a try.

"You can get away from him," Matt suggested in a quiet tone.

Jesse's face reflected sad resignation. "No, no, I can't."

"Dude, you can. You, me, and Trent—we could take Cole and Sokolov. The three of us," Matt stressed in a low voice.

"Not going to happen." Jesse pushed Matt forward.

"At least let me go. Tell them any story you want, make yourself the hero," Matt urged. "Bro, they've got you mixed up in kidnapping, torture ... bail before you sink deeper. Let me escape. I'll stand up for you with the cops. I'll tell them you helped—"

"Shut up!" Jesse grabbed the front of the straitjacket and slammed Matt against the wall. He leaned in. "All I want to do is suit up and hit the field again. That pencil-necked Russian geek in there says he knows people, high in the administration, the Board of Regents even. He promised to convince them to let me back into the university so I can play ball and turn pro. That's all I want. It is the only thing that matters to me."

"But he doesn't—" Matt stopped. He was close enough to pick up Jesse's thought. The desire to return to football was passionate, even desperate. It was the only hope that Jesse clung to; without it, there was nothing but despair. Matt couldn't compete against that. He nodded. "Understood."

Jesse released Matt. They passed the operating room, stopping at the next door. Jesse tapped on it.

Sokolov's voice responded, "Come."

Jesse opened the door and guided Matt inside. The room was featureless and had no windows, most likely storage once. A camping lantern hung from the ceiling, slicing the space into slabs of stark white light and harsh black shadows. Sokolov sat behind a table in a wooden chair that appeared too weak to support him, but he perched there as though he really presided in a CEO's mahogany office instead. Trent, also in a filthy straitjacket, was in a metal folding chair, with an additional one three feet away. Cole stood behind Trent.

"Please take a seat, Matt." Sokolov sounded like the welcoming host to a dinner guest. He waved at the vacant chair.

Matt was a little startled at being called by his proper name. He started to sit but hesitated. He checked the floor first.

Sokolov appeared amused. "No electrical cables. Although after your escape attempt yesterday, you should receive a consequence."

Matt looked at Trent. He smiled in approval. Matt acknowledged him with a nod. "Cole beat you to it."

Cole hissed a satisfied laugh.

"So I understand." Sokolov gestured toward the Black Sedan Boys. "Thank you, gentlemen, that will be all for the present. You may wait outside the door." Jesse bowed slightly before he and Cole left the room. Sokolov again showed the empty seat and smiled. "Please."

Matt glanced at Trent, who shrugged as much as one could while wearing a straitjacket. Matt sat, wondering what Sokolov was up to.

Sokolov pulled the jammer from his pocket and switched it on. He placed it on the table in front of him.

"Commendably cautious," Trent noted dryly.

"A necessity with you two in the room, I think," Sokolov returned. He leaned back in his chair. Matt hoped it would break and send the graduate assistant to the floor. Sokolov regarded Matt and Trent in silence for a moment before he spoke again. "First, I must offer my apologies."

"Oh, you mean for kidnapping us, holding us against our will, and zapping us with electricity?" Matt said. "But, hey. What are small things like that among friends?"

"Matt." Trent's terse message was obvious: *Keep your mouth shut.*

A lightning flash of anger crossed Sokolov's face before being replaced by a smile. It was the indulgent, condescending one used by the lord of the manor to his peasants. "I must admit, my method was a trifle unorthodox. For that, I am truly sorry. In my defense, I found the excitement of studying two with such powers—"

"We don't have any powers," Trent shot back.

"Yeah, especially since my cape is at the dry cleaners," Matt added.

Sokolov cleared his throat and politely chuckled. He leaned towards them, forming a steeple with his slender hands. "Do not underestimate yourselves. Your, well, what should we call it? The ability ... talent ... skill ... you both possess is rare, and I admit I became overwhelmed with the chance to examine such fascinating phenomena at work. Perhaps it led me to be, shall we say, a little too zealous."

Matt opened his mouth. A warning glance from Trent closed it. Matt swallowed what he was about to say. It physically hurt to do so.

Sokolov went on, "I'm surprised your talent, and, I assume, the few others like you, haven't been recognized over the decades. Psychic investigators may not have failed in all of their experiments, but I'm sure a very large number of them did. Then again, I suppose individuals with your ability prefer to keep it a secret, rather than reveal their unique skill to everyone."

"Perhaps they understood what would happen to them if they said anything," Matt spat out as he lifted his shoulders in the straitjacket.

Sokolov ignored the tone of Matt's statement and nodded. "Yes, it could be. Announcing your talent would nullify its value, wouldn't it? Similar to a magician explaining how a trick works to a crowd of people. If your skill is to be useful to you, you must employ it in quiet ... in secret, in the background. Perform it out of sight, in corners, or behind closed doors."

Trent bristled. "Are you suggesting we—"

Sokolov cut him off with a dismissive wave of a hand. "Oh please, don't try to sell me the fiction you never used your skill to your own advantage other than to find the culprit who absconded with the church bingo funds." He was quiet for a moment, glanced between the two, then gave a knowing chuckle. "I never believed you were fools. Just that you merely lacked ambition." He stood. "I must confess my error here," Sokolov flashed a stiff smile, "My original intention in studying your talent was to reproduce it by artificial means. I hypothesized if I duplicated your EEG pattern with the computer, I would recreate your skill. That did not occur. My initial trials were failures. You should be grateful for that, by the way."

"Thankful for your incompetence?" Matt snorted.

"Yes, if you wish to label it thus. I will still pursue the use of the computer. So much simpler that way, and more in my control. However, I am very flexible and prefer as many options open as possible. My lack of success with that process so far is the sole reason you two remain alive to have this discussion." Sokolov's voice was flat and carried the menace of a coiled cobra.

There was dead silence in the room, the obvious implication hanging in the air, as heavy and solid as a wool blanket. Matt spoke it out loud at last. "So, you want us to use our skill to help you?"

Sokolov nodded and leaned back. "Perhaps you are not familiar with the interior workings of the academic world. There is a good deal of politics swirling around a campus. They are frequently petty, but maybe that's the reason they grow so vicious. A position is opening at the university, one which would be a stepping stone to improved opportunities—both inside and outside the higher educational system. However, there is only a limited window for me to take advantage of it."

"What do you expect us to do?" Trent asked.

"As I said, I would like to employ your skills to help me secure this opportunity. I'm sure you can expect there will be other people vying for the same opening. They are not as smart as I, but just as ambitious. Perhaps more so, although I doubt it. I need your assistance to eliminate any competition," Sokolov proposed.

"How are we supposed to do that? Kill them off?" Matt's tone was sarcastic.

"Not that extreme, I assure you. And I wouldn't require you two for that. I could use Cole and Jesse. There are other, less violent, ways," Sokolov spoke in the same relaxed tone. He sat back. "Come, Matt, please. You understand the absurd but critical importance your generation places on social media, particularly of how carefully curated your online identity must be. Using filters on photos, the need for that perfect post, gathering those vital likes. This may be surprising to you, but it is similar for many adults too. No matter how strongly they deny it."

Sokolov chuckled. "Perhaps they never outgrew their adolescence. They still crave the adoration and approval for their self-identified brilliant thoughts posted on various social apps. And, conversely, terrified of appearing not fitting in with the 'cool kids', not being or thinking the same as everybody else, or, worst of all, being tagged as old. This is where your unique talents are come in. Let's say one of my colleagues is in competition for the promotion. You two probe his mind for any undesirable activities he committed in his past or unpopular opinions he holds. Sins for which there is no forgiveness nowadays. There's always something in everybody's past." He shrugged. "You pass the relevant information on to me. We leak our findings on social media or perhaps the mere threat of releasing that data accomplishes the goal; either way, it has the end effect of knocking out a particular competitor."

"You're talking about performing blackmail!" Trent said.

"Yes, of course I am," Sokolov agreed.

Matt couldn't believe what he was hearing. "Wait. This is just for a job promotion?"

"At least initially, but that's only the beginning." Sokolov's eyes blazed. "I present you two with a unique opportunity."

"What is that?" Trent's voice was cautious.

"As I have said, the skill you have gives you an insight into people no one else possesses. You see into their hearts and minds, understand them in a way others cannot. Maybe not even themselves. With this knowledge, you can manipulate them, control them. Maneuver them to do any-thing you want. You can determine both their wants and fears—the carrot and the stick. Employing my set of skills, I'll give you my counsel. With my advice on how to use the data you glean, you can manipulate people to give you your desires. Money, power, sex, whatever you want. At the same time, you are also aiding me to reach my goals." His eyes gleamed with excitement as he leaned forward. "Think of it! The possibilities are limitless!"

Trent and Matt looked at each other, stunned.

"You want us to do what?" Matt sputtered. "You sound like a cheap version of a comic book villain, plotting to take over the world."

"Well, I have the requisite underground lair, as modest as it is." Sokolov glanced around the room and laughed. "But take over the world? Goodness, no! Who wants it? The place is a mess. I don't propose to gain world domina-tion in a similar grandiose manner to those supervillains. I am not that kind of man. No, I am solely interested in acquiring power, pure power. I won't even pretend to wrap it up with a pretty little bow to say it's going to make the world a better place for humankind or save the planet from destruction."

He leaned forward. "No, gentlemen, power is the ends, not the means. The power to control people, make them dance to my tune. I plan to start with small steps, little ones at first. Influence the influencers. Understand their secret, greedy desires and feed them those. Nudge them to say or do the things I ... we ... want. And the lemmings will happily skip along behind them." He chuckled and winked, as though Matt and Trent were in on a joke. "Oh, be sure to take down those who oppose us through the use of innuendo, gossip, and threats. Little by little, our power will grow, and here's the best part: we will be invisible. We remain out of sight, pulling the strings like master puppeteers! All those conspiracy theories people hold, of evil corporations or sinister cabals who control everything, would be correct—except it will be us! Think of what we could do! Imagine the sheer pleasure of pushing and prodding people to do our bidding! Together, we could be unstoppable! Like gods." Sokolov leaned back. "But all that, enjoyable as it promises to be, is merely a proof of concept."

Matt and Trent glanced at each other, puzzled.

"There is a market for our combined skills, gentlemen," Sokolov continued. "Corporations, governments, politicians, all of them would pay dearly to know—actually *know* with absolute accuracy—what their customers or voters think. What their opinions are. It would be the ultimate focus group." He grinned as he patted the jammer. "Of course, we could generate additional funds by selling the means to prevent that. Or being paid not to sell the device ourselves."

"In other words, work both sides of the street," Matt said.

"Precisely," Sokolov responded. "So, what do you say to my little plan?"

Trent and Matt exchanged glances before turning back to Sokolov. "We're not interested," Trent stated.

Matt nodded in agreement.

"What? Why not?" Sokolov asked surprised. "I'm offering you power, wealth, anything you could want!"

"You expect us to work with you? After what you have done to us?" Matt demanded. "How can we trust you?"

"I cannot do this alone! I need your help! This is your guarantee," Sokolov said.

"Help you! Help you pry into other people's thoughts to control them? Be staff assistants to an egomaniac?" Matt fired back. "Cram it, chuckles."

Sokolov's eyes glinted in the harsh, flat light of the lantern. It was as if the face he had worn, of friendliness and pleasantry, was a mask that he removed, folded, and put away like the costume it was. He pulled himself up to his full height. "I understand what I proposed is over-whelming. But I am reasonable. I will give you time to reconsider."

"I'm sure I'm speaking for Matt when I say we will not change our minds," Trent declared as Matt nodded.

"That remains to be seen," Sokolov said and then he called out, "Gentlemen!"

Jesse and Cole entered. At Sokolov's gestures, Jesse took a strap and belted Trent to his chair. Cole pulled Matt to his feet and pushed him toward the door.

"Move it." Cole grabbed one of Matt's shoulders.

Matt shook him off.

"I can walk by myself," Matt grumbled. He stepped into the hallway, followed by Cole. "I guess I'm being sent to time out to think about my inappropriate behavior."

The two started down the corridor. At the intersection, Matt turned toward the padded cells.

"Not that way," Cole ordered as he jerked Matt back. "Straight ahead. We have a different place prepared for your ... thinking."

Matt didn't know his destination, and his nerves tingled. The hallway was long, dim, and appeared to stretch on forever. Through the gloom, he barely could make out old, faded letters painted on the wall at the end of the hall: MORGUE.

He swallowed hard as Cole guided him towards the sign, every step lasting for hours. He reached the door, and a shove pushed through it into the black room. There was a slight click, and another lantern flickered to life.

The room, even after being abandoned for years, still seemed to reek of antiseptic and death. Dirty cracked tiles, at one time a sterile white, lined the walls. Bolted to the middle of the room on a post stood a stainless steel table, a lip running around the edge, and a metal pillow at one end. A drain in the center, used to siphon off bodily fluids, interrupted the smoothness of the top.

Stacked and ordered along one wall were small rectangular doors that resembled a cross between a file cabinet and a refrigerator. One of the metal doors hung open, and a drawer containing a human-sized metal tray was pulled out.

Terror gripped Matt as he realized Cole intended him to be the occupant of the empty container. The thought of being locked up in a locker washed him in an icy panic. It would be like being buried alive. He backed up into Cole.

"No, not in there. Please," Matt begged. "It's like inside a casket ... sealed in a coffin alive. No ... not that. Anything but that. Please ..."

Jesse came into the room.

Matt turned to him. "Jesse ... please ... help me. Tell him to stop ... please ... I can't tolerate small spaces ... please ... help me ... Jesse ..." he pleaded.

"Cole..." Jesse began.

"Shut up and help me, or I'll make sure you go through what these two did on that table. Do you want that?" Cole snarled.

"No," Jesse answered quietly.

Cole removed a rag from the drawer and stuffed it into Matt's mouth. While Jesse took hold of Matt's legs, Cole grabbed him by the shoulders and lifted him off the floor. Matt screamed over and over, but only muffled sobs emerged. He squirmed in their grasp, but they were too strong. They placed him on the tray. Jesse held Matt down by the shoulders while Cole tied his feet together.

"Kick the door three times when you decide to play ball," Cole said. He imitated the tone of a trained customer service representative and added, "Hold, please. We'll get right back to you." Cole slid the tray back into the black, gaping maw of the drawer. He looked in at Matt and grinned. "Sooner or later."

Matt gave a last scream. The outer door slammed closed.

Chapter Sixteen

STRAINING AGAINST THE STRAPS of the straitjacket, Matt was helpless. The constant sound of his heart beating was louder than he'd ever heard before, almost drowning out his screaming. He couldn't see anything but darkness—the darkness of the tomb and death. His hands clenched into fists, gripping handfuls of jacket material as he writhed on the tray. He could sense the walls pressing in, pushing, crushing him. It seemed great lengths of rope that stretched for miles bound his arms and feet together. He stopped struggling at last, exhausted, but the terror refused to release its deadly grip.

He thought of something when he looked at the door. Weren't these lockers airtight, like a refrigerator? Had he used up most of his air with his screaming and fighting? Would he end his life in desperate gasps for oxygen? Drowning in fear, he peered through the darkness past his feet and saw a lighter line around the bottom of the door. The rubber gaskets had broken down after so many years, so there wasn't a tight seal. The gap must permit some air to flow in. He wouldn't suffocate.

That brought him some relief. One of his therapists had taught him relaxation exercises to stop the voices. Of course, it didn't work, but now he used the technique to get himself back under control. He closed his eyes and worked through the steps until he became calm and breathed normally.

He had to think through it. Rationally. Sokolov needed him until he could improve the computer program to duplicate the telepathy skill of him and Trent. Or find other telepaths who would throw in with him. Either of those possibilities would take a while, he reasoned. In the meantime, Sokolov most likely wouldn't follow through on his death threats; he would only do so once he had found someone else or worked out how to understand the thoughts of others himself. Matt figured that would buy him and Trent some time, but he didn't know for how long.

It was pointless to believe that Sokolov wouldn't torture them until they agreed. He had already begun the process. Worse yet, he could hand the task over to the Black Sedan Boys. Cole would probably enjoy the task, and Sokolov would make an appreciative audience, happily munching popcorn while watching the proceedings. Matt saw only one option open to him: agree to work with the Russian, or at least appear to do so. Time to see if Hunter had made an actor of him.

Matt started shrieking in panic again, struggling and fighting inside the locker. He sobbed, he pleaded, and he wailed in anguish. He stopped to catch his breath and listened. No sound came from outside.

The curtain rose on Act 3, and Matt repeated his performance. This time he filled the less hysterical periods with a series of full-force whimpers, with luck sounding heart-rending. Now for the kicker, literally. He bashed the door three times.

No response. Matt became frightened; maybe the Black Sedan Boys had left him alone.

Matt swore under his breath and banged again. That worked. After a minute, the locker swung open, and Cole pulled out the drawer.

"Keep it down! Some of us are trying to get to sleep!" Cole followed his witty remark with his grunting, hissing laughter. He yanked the gag out of Matt's mouth and spoke like a kindergarten teacher. "Have we thought about our behavior during our time out?"

Matt wanted to spit in Cole's face. He couldn't. He needed to play the role of the vanquished. Instead, he nodded. "Take me to Sokolov."

Cole unbound Matt's feet and watched him struggle to sit up, amused. Matt waited, hoping Cole would offer a hand to hop to the floor, but he made no move to assist. Matt jumped to the ground. The pair walked back toward the operating room. They stopped outside, a murmur of voices coming from the other side. Matt remembered Hunter saying he had been so nervous before his first performance that he threw up. Now he understood how Hunter felt.

Cole opened the door, and Matt took a step inside.

Jesse was lying on the gurney wearing the EEG cap and hooked up to the heart monitor. He held a deck of Kenner cards in his hands. Sokolov sat across from him at his laptop. He glared at Jesse like a teacher watching a student fail an exam.

"But the picture shows a star," Jesse insisted apologetically.

"Next one!" Sokolov barked as he stared at the computer screen. Jesse selected the card on top of the stack and looked at it. "Square!"

"No—" Jesse started.

Sokolov growled, then noticed Cole and Matt. He pointed to the gurney and addressed Cole. "Put him there, back to Jesse, two feet away, facing me," he commanded. Cole shoved Matt into the indicated place. "Next one!" He returned his attention to the screen. The rustle of the cards reached Matt. After a second, Sokolov spoke again, "Circle." He shifted his gaze to Matt, expecting him to respond.

Matt shook his head. "Sorry. Wavy lines."

"Jesse?" Sokolov demanded, keeping his eyes fixed on Matt.

"The kid's right. Wavy lines," Jesse answered.

Sokolov scowled at Matt, then snapped his fingers twice. "Next! Next!"

"This is the last one in the deck," Jesse said.

Matt heard the whisper of a card being picked up.

Sokolov stared at the display for a long time. He opened his mouth as though he were about to speak but closed it instead. He paused for a few minutes and squinted at the screen before announcing, "Square."

Everyone turned their eyes on Matt. He nodded. "You are correct. Square."

"What is the card?" Sokolov demanded.

Jesse sounded relieved as he replied, "It's a square alright."

Sokolov looked at the results on the laptop while he tapped some keys. He muttered under his breath, "Accuracy no better than random chance." He stood, faced Matt, and spoke as though everything that had just happened didn't. "So, I assume by your presence you are going to agree to help me with my work?"

Matt cleared his throat. "I agree ... I agree to talk about it. If I get something out of it as well."

Sokolov nodded curtly. "You're a realist." He removed the sensors from Jesse and dismissed the others with a wave.

"Before they go, this needs to come off." Matt shrugged in the straitjacket.

Sokolov hesitated, and Matt went on in irritation, "Look, bro, without this thing on, I'm only wearing my jeans. I don't have a bazooka stuffed down my shorts. At least not a metal one."

The Black Sedan Boys snickered.

"It was a joke." Matt nodded toward Cole and Jesse. "See? Even your goons got it."

"I have little of a sense of humor," Sokolov said with glacial coolness.

"No, no, I suppose you don't," Matt responded.

Sokolov pulled himself up to his full height. "I also wish to remind you that you are in no position to make demands."

"Based on what I just saw, neither are you," Matt said in an even tone. The two locked eyes and stared at each other, their faces impassive. There was a long silence. The faint chug-chug-chug of the generators next door filled in the background.

Sokolov considered for a moment, then nodded. "All right, but if you try anything—"

"Tell you what, I'll sit on the gurney," Matt offered. "I'd be far enough away from you that if I make a move, you can sic your guard dogs on me. Hey, you can even zap me, if you want."

Sokolov signaled to Jesse, who went over to Matt and unbuckled the straitjacket. Once he was free of the constricting garment, Matt rubbed his arms to get the circulation going again. "Thanks Jesse," Matt said.

When Jesse had finished, Sokolov ordered, "You two wait outside."

After the door closed, Matt sat on the gurney, picked up the Zenner cards, and gazed at Sokolov. He returned the look with equal intensity. Matt riffled through the cards.

"That is annoying. Stop immediately," Sokolov snapped.

Matt completed another shuffle and shrugged. He put the deck down, folded his hands on his lap, and looked at Sokolov. His thoughts traveled back to his last session in his final psychologist's office. He worked hard that day to prove he was 'healed'. He had chosen his words cautiously, kept his voice level, and even offered a smile or two to his therapist. On that occasion, Matt's goal was only to spare himself from spending more fifty-minute-hours on the couch. Today he had to do it all over again, but now for something more precious: his life. He began, "Reading people's minds, the greatest thing of all time, right? But not in real life. Sure, I can hear what they're thinking, but their thoughts ..." Matt shook his head in dismay, "it's like being on a bus by a person who insists on using their phone like a walkie-talkie, you know, holding it away from their mouths so everybody has the golden opportunity to listen to both sides of their exciting conversation. Except I can't get off at the next stop. I'm stuck next to them. My ability is a burden, man, having their idiot thoughts clogging up my brain. I'm buried in one huge, smelly, steamy pile of stupid."

Matt glanced at Sokolov. He sat, arms crossed, wearing a blank expression. He said nothing, so Matt plowed on.

"So far, the only thing I could do was tolerate it. And I have ... barely. You were right when you suggested I used my—skill, I believe you call it—for my own good. I have ... some. Mostly for cheating on tests. Little stuff like that." He gave a rueful laugh. "But telepathy still hasn't helped me get a girlfriend."

"You must be frustrated," Sokolov commented with mock sympathy.

And I'm sure you are too, Romeo, Matt thought. He continued, "In more ways than one, dude, in more ways than one. Here's my real frustration. I have this skill that could do so much for me, but I can't use it to my advantage. I might as well be the world's greatest singer in a land of people with no ears." He stopped and took a breath. He gazed at Sokolov with what he hoped resembled admiration. "I don't think like you. You plan. You strategize. I bet you're always at least four moves ahead." He noticed a faint smile from Sokolov. "Not me. Then again, you can't do what I do. Based on what I just saw, you're not even close."

"Yet," Sokolov put in. It sounded like a threat.

Matt nodded in agreement. "Yet, but how long will 'yet' take? You said you didn't have much time, you only had a, like, limited window of opportunity." He leaned forward. "I thought about what you suggested, that we read people's minds, discover their wants and fears, and use that knowledge to control them. Maybe get some cash. A lot of it. I know now that's for me."

"So, you wish to join forces with this 'cheap comic book villain'?" Sokolov mocked.

"Count me in if I get what I want," Matt said.

"To what do I owe this sudden change of heart?" Sokolov probed after a pause.

"Being stuffed into a file drawer used to store dead people concentrates the mind," Matt replied with no trace of sarcasm. "You picked the correct method of ... um, persuasion."

Sokolov stared at him for a long moment before he laughed. Not a pleasant one, but the harsh, gritty laughter of the ungracious victor. He stood, walked to the door, and opened it. He whispered something to the Black Sedan Boys, closed it again, and turned his attention to Matt. "Stand by the wall."

"Okay." Matt hopped off the gurney and moved to where Sokolov pointed. "What's all this about?"

"You'll find out soon enough. This little exercise transformed into an informal experiment on the effectiveness of different persuasion methods. Psychology wins again. Yours was psychological, Trent's was physical."

The door opened. Cole and Jesse shoved Trent into the room. The straitjacket was gone, replaced by a patchwork of black and blue marks across his torso. His hands were tied behind his back, and he was gagged. Cole and Jesse wrestled him to the gurney, securing him down with chest and ankle straps. At Sokolov's gestured command, the Black Sedan Boys left.

Sokolov stepped to the laptop but kept the table between him and Matt. "Come over here."

Matt walked over, trying not to display his uneasiness or glance toward Trent. He attempted to sound breezy. "Okay, I'm here. Now what?"

"Your eloquence has touched me," Sokolov said with smugness, "as well as your stated desire to help me in my work. However, there is something to attend to first."

"And what is that?" Matt failed to keep the suspicion out of his voice.

"A simple task. Do you see the button mounted next to the laptop? The red one?"

"Yes."

"Push it."

"Why? What will that do?" Matt tried to make a joke. "Trigger the self-destruct sequence?"

Sokolov smiled. "No, not at all. It will administer an electric shock to Trent."

"What?" Matt looked toward the gurney.

Trent's eyes showed a combination of fear and pleading.

"I agreed to a demand of yours," Sokolov stated with no emotion. "Now you must agree with one of mine."

"Taking off my straitjacket and ordering me to hurt somebody are two different things," Matt shot back.

"They are indeed." Sokolov clasped his hands in front of him, reminding Matt of an undertaker offering his condolences. He shrugged. "What's your point?"

"It ... like ... it isn't a fair trade!"

"Young man, life is not fair. It never has been and never will be. You will be very disappointed and bitter if you expect life to provide fair trades," Sokolov mocked. "After all, life gave you the power to read minds, but not to other people. That's not quite fair now, is it?"

"Well, no, but ... but ... this is different!" Matt protested.

"How so?" Sokolov tilted his head to the side, studying Matt like he was a unique species of insect.

"Because ... because, like, this is cruel!" Matt held a hand out toward Trent.

"Cruel?" Sokolov cocked one eyebrow. "Cruel? Didn't you just suggest to me how cruel it was for you to be forced to listen to other people's inane thoughts? Did you not tell me you wanted to control people? Earn money from your skill? How did you put it ... 'count you in'?" Sokolov uncrossed his arms and crossed them the other way. "Except you lied, didn't you?"

"No, I didn't." The answer came too fast to be believable. Matt needed to respond calmly to the accusation. He had to convince Sokolov he wanted to join him. It was his only hope for survival. "No. I was not lying."

"So, you are telling the truth?" Sokolov sighed in the same tone as a disappointed parent. "I wish to trust you, Matt. I really do. But I must be certain."

"Look, I ... I don't know what to tell you, bro," Matt sputtered.

"You will do nothing with your mouth," Sokolov said. "People talk but rarely accomplish anything. Those two old sayings are true: talk is cheap, and action speaks louder than words."

"Believe me, I want to help you!" Matt said.

"And you will," Sokolov said softly. "But first, you need to prove to me you're sincere in your offer." He pointed. "You can do so by pressing that button."

"No," Matt said, shaking his head. He moved away from the table. "I won't do it."

"Then I'm afraid this concludes our brief discussion, and you have wasted my time," Sokolov said with regret. "I now will increase the voltage on Trent, slowly, painfully, eventually killing him or destroying his brain, whichever comes first. And you will observe the entire process, knowing you were completely responsible. And it will be a foretaste of your fate."

Sokolov reached over and hit the F3 key on the laptop. A panel appeared on the screen, containing only a simple slider. A number at the top carried the label 'Voltage'.

"You said you couldn't control the strength!" Matt yelled.

"You must have misunderstood my statement. You were in a feeble state at the time." Sokolov moved his hand toward the trackpad.

"No, wait!" Matt called out. His mind raced through all the potential outcomes. They all led to blind alleys. He knew he was engaged in a dangerous game, but he also understood this was what it would take to beat Sokolov. "All right. I'll do it. Whatever it takes to convince you, I'm on your side. Then I'll talk with Trent here, get him to join with us."

Sokolov looked at him, a superior smile on his face. "That's a good boy." He gestured to the button. "Now press the button."

Matt slowly reached for it, his hand trembling slightly. He hesitated.

Sokolov's voice became hypnotic. "Go on. Push it." He turned quiet, commanding. "Think of it, Matt. Think of the power when you control people. There is so much pleasure in it, more than you may be able to possibly endure. Imagine walking among them, listening to their thoughts, with the knowledge they are merely your puppets, your toys, to do with what you wish. Play with them until they irritate or bore you, then discard them. And better still, they won't comprehend your strength. You travel amid them, seen but unseen, yet all-powerful."

Matt's heart raced, and his breath came in short, shallow bursts as he faced his decision. He had done everything he could to avoid causing pain to anyone, even going so far as to putting spiders outside to spare them from the agony of a squashed death. But now, confronted with Sokolov's ultimatum, the only chance he had to save both himself and Trent was to make a terrible choice. He couldn't force himself to perform the ultimate move.

"Power is not given, Matt, it is taken," Sokolov whispered. "Seize it with both hands. Now."

Matt sent a mental message to Trent, *I'm sorry*, even though he knew he wouldn't receive it. He pressed the button.

There was a loud buzzing noise, and Trent convulsed on the gurney, his body arching up in pain as he screamed through the gag. Matt released the key. Trent collapsed back to the table, panting and groaning, glistening with sweat.

"Good, Matt, excellent," Sokolov said in a hushed voice. "Taste the power ... savor it. How sweet it is on the tongue. To be in control of another person's fate. You give out the rewards ... and the punishments. Go on. Push the button again. Again. Display the courage to become a god."

Sokolov's words seemed to crack open a hidden chamber inside Matt's mind, a dark place filled with cobwebs and the malevolent spirits of all the times he had been wronged, forgotten, snubbed, and overlooked. The demons of all these past hurts swirled around him, chattering and demanding vengeance. Matt's face hardened into stone, transforming into the visage of an ancient idol.

Trent looked into Matt's eyes as he pleaded silently. "Please ... no," he wheezed out, even through the gag.

Matt's finger, seemingly with a mind of its own, stabbed the button again.

Trent's body jerked and heaved on the gurney as the electricity pumped into him. His screams echoed off the tiled walls.

Sokolov grinned at Matt. "There. That didn't hurt much, now did it? Power is the single most potent drug in the universe. Everybody craves it, but only a chosen few, we the elite, may partake in it. The response to it is like heroin, though; once taken, nobody feels they should have to give it back voluntarily. It has to be forcibly removed." He gazed at Matt, the proud papa. "Excellent. You and I are truly the same kindred spirits."

Revulsion swept over Matt at the approval. His stomach twisted in nausea. Could he transform into *him*—Sokolov—a soulless, empty corpse posing as a human being? A man cursed always to be lonely, even in the middle of a crowd? Matt backed away from Sokolov, horrified. But he couldn't back away from himself.

Cole burst into the room, Jesse right behind him.

"I told you never to inter—" Sokolov began.

"Shut up!" Cole's harsh whisper cut him off. "Upstairs! Somebody's up there!"

Chapter Seventeen

"WHAT!" EXCLAIMED SOKOLOV.

"Shut up and listen!" barked Cole.

Sokolov, Cole, and Jesse hustled to the doorway, forgetting about Matt. He darted to the gurney and stood with his back to it, as though paying attention to the commotion at the door. He reached behind him and unbuckled the chest strap securing Trent, but he left it in place. He didn't move, blocking the others' view of what he'd done.

Footsteps paced the floor above.

"What do we do?" Jesse's voice edged in panic.

"First off, calm down," ordered Sokolov, "and keep quiet."

Cole whirled around and pointed at Matt. "Not a squeak from you, jerk, if you know what's good for you."

"Oh, I know what's good for me," Matt responded.

"Do you want us to take care of him?" Cole whispered, pointing upstairs.

Sokolov shook his head. "Whoever it is may leave. I don't want to move operations elsewhere. We'll wait quietly."

The visitor's footsteps sounded like soft taps on the wood floor, echoing down the corridor and lingering in the air like a cloud of dust. They reached the top of the stairs. The silence lasted for a few heartbeats, then feet descended several steps. They halted at the locked door.

"Maybe this place is really haunted," muttered Matt.

Jesse appeared a little worried at that possibility.

Cole jabbed his finger at Matt and hissed, "Shut up!"

The unknown visitor tried to open the door, despite the lock, and the knob rattled. After a few seconds, the footsteps retraced their path up the stairs and into the main hall. They traveled down the dense wood floor of the corridor. The entrance thudded closed.

Jesse let out his breath and gave a nervous smile. "That was close. We could have been discovered."

Matt sensed an opening where he could drive in a wedge. He dropped in casually, "No worries, though, Jesse."

"Why not? What do you mean?" Jesse questioned.

"I'm sure Victor has friends in high places who could have smoothed this whole mess over if he needed to," Matt replied. "Isn't that true, Victor?"

That knocked Sokolov off balance, although Matt couldn't tell if it was because of what he said, or that he dared to use Sokolov's first name. In either case, he made a quick recovery. "Of course," he calmed Jesse. "There was no need to worry."

"Sure. All he needs to do is contact his friend on the university Board of Regents," Matt suggested. "Isn't that right, Victor?"

"Yes, yes, I will do that. That is a good idea, Matt." Sokolov's forced smile appeared more like a grimace. He faced Cole and Jesse. "There, gentlemen, you see. Nothing to be concerned—"

Matt snapped his fingers. "Damn, what was his name again? I forgot. I'm lousy at names."

"Wait, that kid knows who the guy is, but you wouldn't tell us when we asked before?" Cole angrily pointed to Matt as he confronted Sokolov.

Matt smiled apologetically and slipped in before Sokolov could answer, "I'm sorry, Victor, my bad. You told me not to say anything to them."

"Don't listen to him! He doesn't know what he's talking about. I didn't inform him of any name," Sokolov assured Cole.

"Then who is the guy?" Cole demanded. "Why not tell us now?"

"You doubt my integrity?" Sokolov huffed.

Matt selected the pronoun carefully. "*We* do."

Sokolov stiffened up like a two-by-four. "This is not the appropriate time to discuss the matter."

"I think it's as good a time as any." Matt knew the Black Sedan Boys were watching the exchange between him and Sokolov, heads swiveling as if spectators at a tennis match.

Sokolov summoned all his dignity. "I'm not at liberty to disclose the individual's name."

"Why not?" Matt lobbed back. "You two aren't sneaking around in the shadows having a torrid love affair or something, are you?"

"No, we are not!" Sokolov roared.

"Why not mention his handle?" Matt pressed. "He is a friend of yours, isn't he?"

"Of course he is!" Sokolov snarled.

"Well, who is he? Is he embarrassed of you, or you of him?" Matt glanced at Cole. He saw the anger bubbling.

"No, nothing of the—" Sokolov returned.

"Then give us his name!" Cole took a threatening step toward Sokolov.

Sokolov hesitated. "Eldon Rivers," he finally answered.

"I'd check that, if I were you," Matt hinted to Cole. He nodded at the laptop. "Do a search."

"Good idea, punk." Cole started toward the equipment table.

"Do not touch that computer!" Sokolov ordered. "There is no internet connection!"

"Well, yes, there is. But I have an easier way to find out." Matt tapped his forehead and took a step in Sokolov's direction. "I'll just read his thoughts. I'm more accurate than a lie detector, anyway. Let me move a little closer—"

"Stay away!" Sokolov backed up, holding up his hands. "Don't you come near me!"

Matt stopped and shrugged. Then he bore in. "By the way, who else is on the Board of Regents? If you know one, you must know the others. At least the names of some members. Who are they?"

Sokolov was at a loss for words. He shot a venomous look at Matt.

"My, my, my! If looks could kill!" Matt folded his arms and leaned against the gurney. "You know what, boys and girls? I don't think Victor here knows anybody on the Board of Regents. Not a single soul." He targeted his next comment at Cole. "He's made a fool of you."

The main door crashed open upstairs. From the hallway, an indistinct voice issued commands. A radio crackled from the opposite end of the corridor, answering the call.

The unmistakable sound of a police scanner, like a storm on a calm day, came in from outside.

"The cops!" Cole swung around, pointing at Matt and Trent. "They did it! They brought them!"

"Hey, it's not us, dude. We're not broadcast towers. We don't have that kind of range," Matt protested, hands spread wide. "But you two are going to have to explain a lot. Especially since Sokolov's so-called friends won't be of any help. Hey, if you're lucky, you all will end up in the same cell. That would be nice and cozy."

The balloon went up as everything happened at once. Swearing, Cole grabbed Sokolov by the front of his shirt while Jesse tried to pull him off. The threesome formed a strange conga line as they backed toward the far wall, Sokolov and Cole shouting at each other, with Jesse imploring them to be quiet.

Matt! Trent's thought broke into Matt's enjoyment of the show. Trent twisted on his side, and Matt untied his hands. *We can deal with Sokolov. You get Jesse, I'll take care of Cole.*

Understood. Matt darted to the end of the gurney to release the straps around Trent's ankles. Just as he finished, he turned in time to see Cole deck Sokolov with a right cross. Jesse fled from the room.

Matt raced after him. He gripped the edge of the doorway and swung into the corridor. Jesse was just taking the corner at the far end. Matt sped up, reached the corner, and used his arms to rebound off the wall to change direction. Jesse hit the bottom of the stairs, and Matt launched into a flying tackle around Jesse's legs. They tumbled to the floor and wrestled. As they rolled in the dust and dirt, a clank of metal on wood resonated through the hall. Matt's hand fell on a pipe. He seized it and wretched it free, bringing it down hard on Jesse's shoulder, Jesse crying out in pain. Matt got to his feet and raised the pipe, ready to deliver another blow, his face twisted with rage.

Jesse lay on his back and stared up at Matt, his eyes wide and frightened. His hands were in front of him in a protective gesture. He spoke, his voice coming out low and plaintive, "Please. I just wanted to play football."

After a second, Matt moved away. "Get out of here." He swung the pipe sideways, showing the stairs. "I said move it!"

Jesse scrambled to his feet and pushed past Matt without a look back. He thumped up the steps, fumbled a bit at the lock, then disappeared through the door, slamming it shut. Matt tossed the pipe to the floor with a loud clang. He turned to run toward the operating room and collided with Sokolov. They simply stared at each other.

Sokolov finally broke the silence, "We don't need them, Matt." He gave a conspiratorial wink. "We can sneak out of here, just the two of us. We can work together."

"I'm sorry I threw down that pipe," Matt said. "I want to bash your head in right about now."

"Step closer, Matt," Sokolov urged. "Read my thoughts. You'll see I'm speaking the truth."

Matt shook his head. "You may have fooled Trent by disguising your thinking, but not me. It doesn't take mind reading to peer behind your tissue-thin thoughts. I can see down all the way to your maggot-infested core ... your true self."

"I saw the expression in your eyes while you shocked Trent. You loved it," Sokolov's voice dropped to a whisper, "Your inner self is more similar to mine than you care to believe, my young telepathic friend. But you refuse to use your power, crippled by your ideas of morality and fair play. Therefore, you are insignificant and small. You will always remain thus."

"It's better than playing the fool for somebody else's dream." Matt glanced down and noticed Sokolov carrying the laptop containing all the information about Matt, Trent, and the experiments. He grabbed it. "I think I'll take this."

The two struggled over the device like toddlers fighting over a toy.

Suddenly, a voice came from upstairs, "Frank! Joe! Over here!"

Distracted, Sokolov looked up, and Matt wrenched the laptop from his grip. Matt smiled sweetly. "Must you go? I think the police would like to have a word with you. Kidnapping, it would be."

Sokolov dashed up the stairs and threw open the door. The beam of a powerful flashlight hit him square in the face. Startled, Sokolov backed up and held up a hand to block the glare from his face. He steadied himself before he almost tumbled down the steps. On the other side of the doorway stood a figure in dark blue pants and a lighter blue shirt, a pinned-on badge glinting in the reflected light. Red and blue flashing lights bounced off the walls.

"Excuse me, sir," Hunter said, "I'm working my way through the police academy, and I'm selling subscriptions to *Real Cases—*"

Another blast of police calls echoed down the stairs. In a panic, Sokolov shoved Hunter to one side and ran up the steps.

"Hunter! Don't let him escape!" Matt cried.

"Officer Hardy! Here he comes!" His friend took off in pursuit. "Sir! Sir! I'm also selling delicious chocolates!"

Matt spun around and charged back down the corridor. Rounding the corner, Cole staggered backwards out of the operating room door and crashed into the opposite wall. He looked like a loser from a bar fight: his shirt was almost torn off and blood dripped from his mouth. Trent followed closely after him and delivered a series of punches to Cole's face, knocking him out cold. Cole slid to the floor.

Matt ran up to Trent and viewed the prostrate form lying at his feet. "Looks like you've done that before."

"A few times," Trent gasped out while he caught his breath. He wiped his mouth with his right fist. "Sometimes cowhands need things explained to them. And bullies don't know what to do when somebody fights back."

Matt put down the laptop. "Let's lock him up."

"Where's the police?"

"I think it's a force of many being imitated by one. I'll tell you later," Matt dismissed. "We need to take care of something first."

Trent grabbed Cole's feet and dragged the unconscious body down the hall. Matt sprinted ahead and opened the door to his padded cell. Trent deposited Cole inside, then locked the door. Matt jogged back to the computer.

"Wait ... take care of what?" Trent called after him.

Matt scooped up the laptop and stepped into the operating room. It was a mess. The gurney was jammed against the wall. The equipment table had been overturned, and the EEG and heart rate monitors laid haphazardly across the tile floor. Pens and pieces of paper lay scattered about. "Wow. You two weren't fooling around."

"It wasn't exactly the church social," Trent said as he followed Matt in. "What happened to Jesse and Sokolov?"

"I let Jesse go. I don't know about Sokolov yet." Matt righted the table and placed the laptop on it. Trent opened his mouth to say something. Matt stopped him. "I have to deal with this drive first."

"On the computer? How come?"

"Look, dude, all our personal info, including Sokolov's notes about us and his experiments, are stored in this thing." Matt waved a hand toward the laptop. "We need to delete the files before the cops examine them."

"So? They won't have a clue what any of it means. It won't make any sense to them," Trent said.

"Probably not, but they could hand the data over to somebody who could figure it out ... like the government. Guess what our lives would be if the CIA got hold of this information and checked it out," Matt said as he opened the laptop's lid. "They've already tried the remote viewing thing with no success. Now think about what they would do if they discovered it really could work. With us." He snorted. "Not only that, but they'd also give Sokolov a job overseeing the entire project."

"Well, we can hide it and fiddle with it later."

"Sokolov certainly will tell the cops about the laptop," Matt said. "It would make it weird if it vanished, and we were the only ones with access to it. That's a tad obvious. I have to deal with it now."

"Why not just smash the thing? It could have happened during the fight," Trent suggested.

Matt shook his head. "That would still leave any back-ups."

Hunter's voice echoed from the hall, "Matt!"

"In here!" Matt called. He switched on the laptop and stepped back to avoid being overwhelmed by the boot sequence flooding his brain.

Hunter limped into the room. "Sorry. That guy got away. He fights dirty."

"Figures." Matt's eyes remained glued to the computer.

"But I have his picture and one of his car's license plate!" Hunter held up his cell phone.

Matt gave a thumbs up. "Oh, Hunter, Trent. Trent, Hunter." He gestured between the two.

"Pleased to meet you," Trent said, a little bewildered.

"Hey. So, you're like the other mind reader guy?" Hunter asked.

Matt responded to Trent's questioning look. "It's okay. He knows."

"Yeah, in the flesh." Trent gazed at Hunter's outfit doubtfully. "So ... are you with the police?"

"No, he's an actor," Matt clarified.

"I wore this costume when I played Officer O'Hara in a scene from *Arsenic and Old Lace* for drama class," Hunter said.

"Oh." Trent sounded like he still didn't quite understand. "But I heard voices ..."

"Hey, Matt told you. I'm a thespian." Hunter cleared his throat and spoke in a deeper voice, "Joe! Frank! Over here!" He pulled one of his walkie-talkies out of his pocket, held it close to his lips, and mumbled something. The other radio crackled from upstairs. He showed his phone. "The police call stuff is from the scanner app I downloaded. I rigged up a couple of LED lights I have outside to flash red and blue, just like a cop car. Pretty good for a one-man show, eh?"

"Take your bows later. Now, Hunter, you get to do what you wanted to ever since the start," Matt announced.

"Call the cops?" Hunter asked in an eager voice.

Grinning, Matt pointed his finger at Hunter like giving a cue. "You're up. Phone the men in blue."

"Oh, boy! I'm going outside for a stronger signal! I'll give them Sokolov's license plate and everything!" Hunter rushed from the room.

"None of this makes any sense ..." Trent said under his breath, watching Hunter leave.

Matt scowled at the screen and swore. "Of course it's password protected."

Trent turned his attention back to Matt. "Did you expect anything else?"

Matt shrugged.

"Well, since the password is unknown to us ..." Trent held up one hand in defeat. "We're stuck."

Matt's eyes fell on the EEG. An idea began to form. "I may get it to work ..." he said to himself.

"Get what to work?"

"I hope the fall didn't break this gizmo." Matt lifted the EEG off the floor and set the machine next to the laptop.

"Are you saying you can hack into the laptop?" Trent said. "With an EEG?"

"In a way. At least, I think so." Matt attached the cables from the EEG to the laptop. "I can connect to computers and read the minds of CPUs."

"You can what!" Trent sputtered.

"Read a CPU. Understand the contents of the chips and what they're thinking—if it's called that." Matt paused for a moment, staring at nothing as he sifted through his conclusions before continuing, "Perhaps telepaths are like, maybe, members of a track team. One guy is good at sprints, while another runs the mile, but they're both runners. We're both telepaths, but we have unique skills ... specialties. You have a range of four or five feet. I can understand the thoughts of a computer chip, although I haven't figured out how it works completely. I may be limited to certain types of chips, or they must be running a specific operating system, or I don't know what else ..." Matt finished with the cables and straightened out the wire leads. "Remember, I told you I believed that Sokolov's modifications to the EEG increased our telepathic strength when we were hooked up?"

Trent nodded. "Yes."

"The other CPUs I interfaced with were unlocked, but not this one. I'm thinking the power boost from this EEG will help me break into the laptop, no password required ... like a battering ram through a door. At least, I hope so. Once I'm inside the CPU's mind, I'll see what damage I can do to the files," Matt explained.

"Are you sure that will work?" Trent sounded doubtful.

Matt handed the sensor cap to Trent and grinned. "Not in the least."

"Is it ... is it safe?" Trent asked in a concerned voice.

"No idea. I didn't spend more than a few minutes in communication with a computer before." Matt recalled the unease he had after the first journey into his laptop. He pushed that out of his mind as he moved the gurney back to its original position and hopped on. "There's just one way to find out, and I need to before the cops get here." He lied down and pointed at the cap. "Wire me up."

Trent hesitated, then snugged the cap on Matt's head. He returned to the EEG, running his hand along the connecting wires to keep them untangled. "I'm only going to turn this on. I won't touch any of the other controls."

"That should be enough." Matt laid his arms over his chest, almost like a corpse in a coffin, and gazed up at the roof.

"Ready?"

"Ready as I'll ever be," Matt said.

He took a deep breath and closed his eyes.

"Best of luck." Trent switched on the EEG's power.

Chapter Eighteen

MATT FLOATED AGAIN IN that different, dimensionless cosmos. As before, he was a creature of energy with no physical form. He flowed serenely through this universe as though on a calm stream, viewing the bursts of energetic light surrounding him. They merged into a rainbow spectrum, pulsing and burning bonfires, exploding like fireworks. Color saturated his brain. The shapes contained texture and bulged as though rippling water. Blue and green spiraled together in visions of distant galaxies. Among all this, he sensed Trent's mind, as well as the electronic presence of the EEG and the laptop.

As beautiful as everything was, Matt realized he needed something stronger, more concrete to anchor to what flowed around him. Just as he did with his own computer, he concentrated, seized the colors and light, and began to mold them in a familiar setting. At last, a hallway, stretching into infinity, took shape. The walls, floors, and ceiling consisted of white, shiny marble. Doors of every type, from barns, vaults, houses, and factories, composed of wood, metal, or plastic, lined the corridor. Although he couldn't detect any source of illumination, everything was bright. This was a place he understood he could function in.

He wandered down the stone passage. Most of the doors didn't display nameplates or any other form of identification. He came to a half-glass, half-wood one resembling those he saw at the Sleep Clinic. Neatly lettered on the pebbled glass was 'EEG'. No need to peek in there. Next, he reached a wooden door, which looked like it came from a stable. Painted in chipped, brown, block letters was 'Trent'.

He continued, finally halting by the door he wanted, surrounded by an iron frame in the shape of a scholar's desk lamp. It had a large book embossed on the front, with 'Laptop' written boldly on the volume's cover.

Somehow, Matt understood that his current form of pure energy wouldn't help him get him past that barrier. He concentrated again, picturing himself with the physique of a superhero. His body grew and expanded, his limbs lengthened, and his muscles tightened and bulged. He was strong, mightier than he had ever been before, and he could run a marathon to win the gold or power lift a ton.

He grasped the doorknob, amused at the size of his hand, muscular forearm, bulging biceps, and the green color of his skin. He smiled to himself. *After all this, watch the door be unlocked,* he thought. He twisted the handle and pushed.

It didn't budge.

He turned to his side. Widening his stance, he lowered his shoulder and charged forward. He smashed into the door and felt some vibrations, but nothing else: no sound, and, thankfully, no pain from the impact. Four times he crashed into it with no effect. On his fifth try, the lock unexpectedly burst open, dumping him on the floor inside.

On the other side was a strange type of office. One wall contained a row of metal file cabinets, lined up like soldiers. The opposite side consisted of electronic panels, bristling with flashing lights and switches, seemingly pulled from the space ship set of a sci-fi movie. The third housed an old-fashioned telephone switchboard: a tangle of cables, plugs, and sockets. In the center of the area stood a wood teacher's style desk, complete with an ancient typewriter.

Matt climbed to his feet. The room glitched and pixelated like a damaged image file rendered on a computer screen. He concentrated again, and the office stabilized. He required a great deal of mental energy to maintain this world and didn't know how long he could keep everything formed. His task needed to be accomplished rapidly.

Moving to the file cabinets, he opened a drawer, and using both hands, yanked out the files and flung them in the air. The folders left his hand as though shot from a gun. They hit the ceiling, the floor, and the walls and scattered in every direction. He did the same to the next drawer, and the next, and the next, until fluttering pieces of paper swirled around him like autumn's falling leaves.

He hustled to the switchboard, unplugged all the connections, then yanked out the cords by their roots as though they were weeds. He flung them to the floor and kicked them across the room.

The office twisted and fractured, tiny sections shattering and becoming lost in a fog. Matt staggered back to the desk and collapsed into the chair. His mind was drained, impossibly so. He had only a few seconds to finish. He pushed himself to his feet and summoned the last ounce of his strength, picked up the typewriter, and hurled it at the wall of blinking lights.

A direct hit. The middle panel split down the center as though a sheet of torn paper. Bundles of wires spilled out like guts. Sparks leaped from the other panels, and they went dark.

Bright red light, churning and moving like a thundercloud, filled the space. Matt instinctively held up his arms to protect his face, but they were gone. The physical body he pictured, as well as the world he'd sculpted with his thoughts, vanished.

Again, he transformed into the being of energy, or perhaps it was only his soul, now floating in an absolutely black void. His mind probed through the darkness, searching for Trent's consciousness or any signs of life. He'd even settle for the signals from the EEG. Nothing came back. There were no sensations. The space was uninhabited, completely devoid of anything or anybody else. He was utterly alone and lost in this nothingness of non-existence. The emptiness frightened him. How long would he be stranded here? All eternity?

Some other energy, or being, or consciousness, or something materialized. It seemed to be far away, but Matt sensed peace flowing from it. He started floating in its direction, but suddenly his movement stopped. The other presence, while not exactly rejecting him, didn't seem ready to receive him yet, as though he was too early for an appointment.

A sharp jolt of pain shot through him. He wasn't bothered by it; at least it reminded him perhaps he was still human, still alive.

The sensation of falling from a height began after a second stab of agony. A rough, rushing wind gathered against his back, and he grew aware of having a physical body again. The air resistance buffeted him, as though he was in a free fall from an airplane. His speed increased. He came to an abrupt stop when he felt he'd slammed into something hard.

There was a sharp intake of breath, then he breathed, deep and evenly. After a while, he opened his eyes. Trent and Hunter stood next to the gurney, looking down at him with sad, concerned faces.

"Hey." Matt gave a weak smile. "Why the gloomy looks? I'm not dead."

Hunter and Trent returned the grin.

Trent clasped Matt on his shoulder. "I'm sorry about the electrical shocks. When I turned on the EEG, it automatically started recording." Trent was quiet for a moment, then tightened his grip. "You flat-lined. I didn't know what else to do."

Matt shivered. That empty limbo he inhabited was a taste of death. He shook himself out of the feeling. "Got it. Thanks, but twice? I thought maybe you were getting back for what I did to you earlier."

"Well, there's that," Trent admitted with a lopsided grin.

"What about the laptop?" Matt propped himself up on his elbows.

Trent waved one hand toward the computer. "It's toast. Literally. Blue smoke and everything."

Matt slowly sat up. Both Trent and Hunter held their hands out as though ready to catch him if he toppled over. "Cops?"

"On their way." Hunter saluted.

Matt turned to his friend. "How long have I been here? Missing?"

"A little less than two days," Hunter said.

"Wow. It seems way longer." Matt shook his head and scrubbed his hair with his fingers.

"When I didn't hear from you and I couldn't reach you, I decided it was action time," Hunter said.

"How did you discover us?" Matt asked.

"From your computer," Hunter replied. "You were using the web version of the 'find your phone' app. I simply checked your browser history and pulled up the map. The pin was stuck here. I drove around back." He showed locations with his hands. "Your car. Tree branch. You should have just left a sign saying 'entrance'."

"Wait a minute," Matt said, "you said on my laptop? In my room? At my house?"

"Of course." Hunter nodded.

"But I locked up before I left. I'm sure I did," Matt insisted.

His friend smiled. "Your memory is fine. You did. I just, um, let's say I let myself in."

"You broke into my house!" Matt accused Hunter with a laugh.

"Well, yeah, you might say that," Hunter said cautiously. "By the way, I owe you for a new garage window."

"Nobody saw you do that?" Trent asked.

"I was wearing my ninja costume," Hunter said like it was the most obvious thing in the world.

Trent and Matt exchanged glances. "He's an actor," they said simultaneously.

"Oh, and I fed Sushi some wet food," Hunter put in. "She was loud and persistent."

Matt grinned. "Thanks. At least you have your priorities straight. Save the cat." Matt gestured for Hunter to continue. "All right, that gets you in my house, but how did you get into my account? My laptop must have logged me out. You don't know my PIN."

"You never changed the default password for the administrator." Hunter waggled a finger at him. "Terrible security. Naughty, naughty boy. But I forgive you in this case. I just signed on as the admin and had access to everything."

"So you were upstairs at the basement door earlier?" Trent asked.

"Oh, I was here much longer," Hunter said. "I scoped out the entire building, top to bottom until I reached that door. That seemed a little funny, a new lock in a place like this. Then came a couple of screams."

"That would have been me," Trent cast a glance at Matt. "But we only heard you on the stairs."

"That's because I meant you to," Hunter explained with a shrug. "I made sure I was extra noisy on the steps and slamming the outside door, then I sneaked back to listen. We actors know how to move quietly in the dark. We do it backstage all the time. After I returned, I heard voices down here, so I set up for my grand entrance. Placed one radio at the far end of the hall and my phone with the police scanner app turned up real loud. I wanted to see if I could shake things up. I guessed it worked."

Matt applauded. "Bravo! Bravo!"

Still a little confused, Trent joined in the clapping. Hunter grinned and took a deep theatrical bow. He imitated a hammy Shakespearean performer, "Thank you! Thank you very much! You are far too kind! And now, I must take my leave and go yonder whilst I await the arrival of the gendarmes." He bowed again and made a grand exit.

Trent turned to Matt after Hunter left. "He's unlike anybody I've met before ..."

"Not even in the desert?"

Trent shook his head in amazement. "Not even in the desert."

Matt chuckled. "I'm proud to call him a friend."

"We need to decide what we're going to tell the police, Matt." Trent sat next to Matt on the gurney. Not knowing when Hunter would return, and wanting to keep their conversation confidential, the two moved into telepathic communication.

Why not the truth? Matt began.

Trent looked startled. *That Sokolov kidnapped us because we can read minds?*

Matt shook his head. *No, that Sokolov kidnapped us because he dreamed up this nutty idea that we can read minds.*

Trent faced Matt and grinned.

The evidence is gone, Matt said. *I wiped the computer files, and I'm sure I nailed the backups as well. It's just his word against ours.*

And we don't have to prove we are telepathic unless we want to. Which we don't. Trent nodded in approval. *You understand this will make Sokolov look insane.*

Isn't he?

Trent laughed as he moved back to verbal speech. "I mean, thinking we can read minds!"

Matt joined in. "Really. How silly is that!"

The sound of an approaching siren drifted through the air.

"Stay in range when the cops are here," Trent said. "Then our stories will match."

"Agreed. We don't need to worry about Hunter saying anything. I'll talk with him." Matt noticed something on the floor. It was sticking out from under the corner of the paper. Like a falcon swooping down on a mouse, he hopped off the gurney and pick the item up: the neuro-pul-somatic-jammer. He slipped into his pocket and looked at Trent. "You didn't see that."

Trent shrugged. "See what?"

Matt and Trent stepped out of the front door of Matt's home. Trent shifted into spoken language; they had used both speech and telepathy for the past two days. "Thanks for letting me bunk at your place while we dealt with the police and the DA."

"Of course. It helped they deposed us in tiny offices next to each other. Quite easy to stay in touch," Matt said. "You know, the more we gave statements, the more unreal the whole thing became."

"Imagine how it will make Sokolov sound when he tries to sell them on our being telepathic," Trent chortled.

"A total nut case," Matt said. "Although, in some ways, I feel sorry for him. I sat at the same table once."

"You didn't do what he did," Trent pointed out.

"Yeah, I guess you're right," Matt agreed. "He's reaping what he sowed, or whatever the expression is."

"That's it."

"If he goes to trial, you can stay here again," Matt said. "I'm sure my mom and dad would like to meet you."

"Are you positive you don't want me to hang on a few more days to help?" Trent offered. "You were on the phone with your parents a long time last night."

"Yeah, I wanted to wait until I got them home before telling them, but a nosey neighbor saw the news report on TV. She decided it was her duty to be the first to let them know." Matt shrugged. "I can handle them. Been there, done that. I'll do it again, but thanks for the offer."

"Are they freaked?" Trent asked.

"That's mild. I wonder if they saved any of my old medications. They may need to take them." Matt chuckled. "I worked hard to calm them down enough not to change their flight home. They mean well."

They reached Trent's truck. Trent opened the passenger door and tossed in his suitcase. He slammed the door, and the two walked to the driver's side.

"I'm sure I'll be rushed back into therapy so I can 'process' what happened to me. I don't know." He shrugged. "Maybe this time I'll listen to what the psychologist is saying, rather than plotting to outfox him."

"Good idea."

"How long will it take to drive to your ranch?" Matt asked.

"About a day." Trent settled into the seat, and Matt leaned on the door. "I can't wait to see the old place again. I figured out my heart is really there. The longer I'm gone, the more I miss it."

Matt picked up an image in Trent's mind. He grinned. "And the brunette who works at the grocery store. Brandi, is it?"

"I forgot. No secrets from you. Get away from me." Trent lightly pushed Matt from the door with one hand. He smiled. "Well, yes, you're right. I think she's interested in me."

"Dude, you've read her thoughts. You *know* she is!" Matt laughed.

Trent flushed a deep red and cleared his throat. "Okay, there's that, but I also can't wait to get back out on the range. Land spreading out all around you ... the mountains, purple in the distance, that endless blue sky over your head. Matt, it's so ... so magnificent. It's almost beyond words to describe the feeling. It's you, the earth, and God."

"Awesome. I'd like to see it one day."

"Tell you what, why don't come out over your winter break? Weather permitting, or even if it's not, I'll get you up on a horse," Trent said.

"For reals?" Matt beamed. "Yeah, count on it!"

"And before you ask, yes, Hunter can join you, too," Trent added.

"I'm sure he'd like that. I don't think he's ever played the role of a cowboy before. Of course, he'll need an appropriate costume," Matt said.

"Tell him we got plenty. Authentic, too." Trent pulled a pad and pencil out of the glove box, then scribbled something down. He tore off the page and handed it to Matt. "Here's my address and phone number. Write to me when you know the dates."

"Write?"

"Yes. You know, write. With a pen and paper, envelope, stamp," Trent said with a smile. "Cell service is spotty out there."

"How prehistoric." Matt read what Trent wrote. "Like, does the Pony Express stop by once a week?"

"Only if a dinosaur didn't eat the rider," Trent returned. "I think you'll enjoy it on the ranch. It'll be a nice break before you head off to college."

"I'm not sure I want to go to college," Matt said. "Mom and Dad have decided. I haven't. I'm not really sure what I want to do."

"There's no law you have to go college straight out of high school," Trent said. "If you like ranch life, then consider spending the summer working with us after you graduate. You're welcome, and we can always use the help. Though I warn you, it won't be a vacation. It's a lot of hard physical work, but it would be good for you. You'd earn some cash, plus pack some muscle on that skinny frame of yours. And plenty of time to plan what you want to do next."

"Just me, the earth, and God. I like the sound of that." Matt paused, then laughed. "I can just see my parent's faces when I tell them I'm going to work as a cowhand."

"Ranching is an honorable profession." Trent sounded a little defensive.

"I know it is, but it doesn't give my parents any bragging rights. I know, I'll tell them I'm going to be a 'bovine engineer'. That will do it." Matt grinned. "But I have to get through my senior year first." He patted his pocket. "With the jammer, it'll be a cinch. At least until the battery dies."

"You haven't let that thing out of your sight since you took it." Trent warned, "Don't become dependent on it."

"You sound like a big brother," Matt joked.

"Are you offering me the position?"

Matt was quiet for a second and gently kicked the ground with a sneaker. Finally, he answered, "Yeah … yeah, I guess I am."

"I accept your offer gladly," Trent said in a crisp manner.

Matt looked up at Trent and smiled. "Sweet. I mean, we have the same eye color. We must be related."

Trent laughed. "My first big brotherly duty is to remind you of something." He turned serious. "We can't control being telepathic, Matt. It just happened to us. The only thing in our power is how we react to it."

Matt took a deep breath. "I know, I know. You're right, but it will be hard."

"You want a pass because it will be hard? Difficult? Life's a struggle," Trent said. "You can do it. You possess the strength. Look at what you survived."

"I'll try," Matt said. He corrected himself, "No, no. I'll do it."

"Exactly what I want to hear." Trent started the truck and reached his right hand out of the window.

Matt stepped up and grasped it. He looked into Trent's eyes. *Stay safe, my brother.*

Trent shook Matt's hand. *You too, my brother. See you in December.*

Matt backed away from the truck. The two exchanged waves, then Trent drove off. Matt watched until the red pickup truck turned the corner.

Walking inside his house, he went up to his room and stood still for a moment. He pulled the jammer out of his pocket and turned it over in his hand. He opened the top drawer of his dresser and slid the device, all the way to the back, under his clothes. With a satisfied smile, he pushed the drawer shut.